Books on Demand

Brigitte Gschwandtner and her husband Hermann live in a small town in Germany. Their children have all left home by now and live in different countries; the Gschwandtners have several grandchildren. The couple served as pastors and missionaries for over forty years. These experiences have helped create her stories. She has published nine novels so far and also translates books from English into German.

Brigitte U. Gschwandtner

Glimpses of Christmas

From Around the World

© 2016 by Brigitte U. Gschwandtner
Translated from German by Brigitte, Dorothea and Rebekah Gschwandtner
Original title: Das Licht reist um die Welt
Cover design by Dorothea and Johannes Gschwandtner

Produced and published in Germany by BoD – Books on Demand GmbH, Norderstedt

All rights reserved. No part of this publication may be reproduced, stored in a retrieval system, or transmitted in any form or by any means-for example, electronic, photocopy, recording-without the prior written permission of the author and the publisher. The only exception is brief quotations in printed reviews.

ISBN 978-3-7392-4651-2

This is a work of fiction. Names, characters, incidents and dialogues are, unless otherwise indicated, products of the author's imagination and are not to be construed as real. Any resemblance to actual events or persons, living or dead, is entirely coincidental.

Table of Contents

Advent			6
This Book ...			7
1:	Mary	– Nazareth, Israel – under Roman rule	9
2:	Shobana	– Lonach, Sri Lanka – ca. 2006	14
3:	Ulrike	– Lüneburg, Germany – ca. 1975	19
4:	Fahmida	– Seeran Valley, Pakistan – 2005	23
5:	Filipe	– Lisbon, Portugal – 1978	26
6:	Kendrick	– Vancouver, BC, Canada – 2013	30
7:	Gergana	– Sofia, Bulgaria – ca. 1998	35
8:	Pedro	– Ecuador – ca. 2003	39
9:	Eruera	– Wanaka, New Zealand – ca. 2004	44
10:	Sentwali	– Massai-Amboseli, Kenya – ca. 1982	49
11:	Amol	– Washim, India – 2003	53
12:	Joseph	– Jerusalem, Israel – under Roman rule	56
13:	Calum	– Isle of Lewis, Scotland – ca. 1965	62
14:	Caitlin	– Isle of Lewis, Scotland – ca. 2000	66
15:	Lydia	– Cape Town, South Africa – 1982	70
16:	Harimaya	– Khani, Nepal – ca. 1990	74
17:	Jean-Luc	– Haiti – ca. 1980	77
18:	Tatyana	– Upper Volga River, Russia – ca. 1993	81
19:	Khaya	– Bulawayo, Zimbabwe – ca. 2000	86
20:	Binoy	– Naogaon, Bangladesh – ca. 2004	90
21:	Flavia	– Cuernavaca, Mexico – ca. 2001	94
22:	Marit	– Kiruna, Northern Sweden – ca. 1995	98
23:	Govind	– Mumbai, India – 1998	103
24:	Bela	– Bethlehem, Israel – under Roman rule	107
Acknowledgments and Resources			111

Advent

Can you see how
Advent is here?
Get ready now
For Christmas cheer.

You decorate front yards
And put up the tree.
You plan meals and cream tarts,
You're busy as a bee.

You haste through the crowds in the mall
While Christmas songs sound everywhere.
You search for nice presents for all:
A doll and a toy train and bear.

>
> Father, did you have all this in mind
> When you sent your only Son to us?
> How we must have grieved your loving heart
> When we changed your gift to such a fuss.
>
> Help us, God, to reconsider this.
> Let us understand what your gift meant.
> Open our eyes to what's amiss.
> Make us see your grace and then repent.
>
> God chose to be born an infant boy,
> Left the heav'nly glory far behind,
> Lived like us on earth in grief and joy
> Brought salvation, healed the lame and blind.
>
> God in diapers! Do I year by year
> Use the manger as an ornament?
> Do I just adore a baby dear
> And his gift I do not comprehend?

This Book ...

... was written over a long period of time. It started within our local church where for several years a children's story was read during the Christmas Eve service. As I had already published some books it seemed natural for me to write those stories myself. By the time the congregation changed their program to include other program items, I had already accumulated a small stock of stories on which to build.

Due to our missionary work my husband used to travel to many different countries, and once in a while I accompanied him. On these journeys I was able to collect additional material for my stories. But most countries change over time. That's why I have added a date behind the title of each story in the table of contents to indicate in what kind of surroundings they are set. To give an example: I traveled to India in the years of 1999 and 2006 and visited Kanjur Slum in Mumbai and also the hospital in Washim. During my first visit, the fuel-run three-wheelers had no catalytic converters yet and their exhaust produced black tails of smoke, as I describe in the story of Govind which I wrote in December 1999. When I returned in 2006, those "tails" were gone.

Some details, especially in the stories of Mary and Joseph, may seem strange. Over the centuries, discoveries have been made that changed things we took for granted but which had been invented later. One example is Joseph's profession. He built houses, which in his area at his time were mainly made from stone, sometimes hewn into rocks. As there were extensive forests in northern and central Europe, many houses were built from wood. So folklore during the Middle Ages turned the original mason into a carpenter.

Many of the stories are fictitious. But they could easily have happened like that, and the general circumstances such as the war of independence in Mozambique or the earthquake in Pakistan are historically correct. Several friends and coworkers in the respective countries—mainly locals—gave me detailed information and thus helped me make the stories as authentic as possible. I'm especially grateful to these brothers and sisters in the faith.

I have included 24 stories on purpose. This way the book can be used as a missionary and literary Advent calendar. No matter how you read it: I wish you the blessing, joy and peace of him whose incarnation we celebrate at Christmas.

Yours in the Lord,
Brigitte U. Gschwandtner

1: Mary
Nazareth, Israel – under Roman rule

Busily she kneaded the dough for the flat bread. Then she suddenly stopped and listened. From one moment to the next it had become strangely quiet in the adjoining workshop. No sound of chiseling or hammering! Was something wrong?

While she turned to her dough again, she heard a man's voice. That wasn't Joseph's voice! But then Joseph answered. For some time both men talked quietly to each other but she couldn't understand a single word.

Then the door to the workshop opened, and Joseph entered. His face was grave with a deep frown on his forehead. He stepped over to her and asked, "How quickly can you get ready for a trip?"

"A trip?" Her eyes moved over her body, and she put a hand on her belly in which the child had now been growing for over eight months. Then she looked up again, a silent question in her eyes.

"I'm sorry, Mary." He took a deep breath. "The Roman emperor has ordered a census."

"What does that mean? Why do we have to travel for that? And where to?"

"Everybody has to go to the town of his forefathers. As I am a descendant of David I have to go to Bethlehem."

"To Bethlehem? Ohhh!"

"Yes. I'm very sorry to have to make you do such a long journey just now. But we are powerless against the Roman oppressors. There's no other way than to go. How soon can you be ready?"

Mary stared down at her dough and contemplated. "Early tomorrow morning? Would that be okay? Or do we need to leave today? I should pack a few things and finish this bread."

"Okay, tomorrow morning then. That gives me a little time to finish one task and put the workshop in order. We'll be gone for quite a while."

"Yes, Joseph!" Sighing, Mary turned back to her kneading. While she was working she considered what she could take along in terms of food. There were still some raisins, a little flour and several dried figs. If she hurried she could bake a cake out of that. They could live on it for several days.

She had little else. It wasn't very long ago that Joseph had taken her into his home. The wedding had actually been planned for a later date. But the child had altered all their plans.

A warm surge of gratitude towards Joseph rushed through Mary. He had had a very good reason to report her to the authorities and, if the Romans allowed it, even have her stoned to death when he discovered her pregnancy. At first it looked like it. She could well remember his shocked and disappointed face when her linen garment could no longer hide her growing belly. Without a word he had turned around and stumbled away.

But on the very next day he had come back. A little shyly he had smiled at her, taken her by the hand and said quietly, "Come with me!" And she had followed him without any hesitation.

Only many days later he had told her what had induced him to act like that. The same angel Gabriel who had appeared to her had told him in a dream at night whose son it was that was growing inside her. Now also Joseph knew, and they kept their secret like a precious treasure.

Early the next morning they left Nazareth. Mary turned around, casting a last look towards the town. Then she followed Joseph and they descended into the valley.

If they could have walked fast they might have reached the Jordan valley by evening. But Joseph didn't want to tire Mary out in her condition. In a little village he knocked at the door of a fellow mason whom he knew. Benaiah and his wife Eglah readily took in the two travelers and prepared a bed for them.

On the following day Joseph and Mary again set out early to cover a good distance before the clouds that had gathered during the night drenched them with a heavy downpour. In Beth Shean, where several trade routes crossed, they turned into the Jordan valley. Joseph let Mary rest at the village well while he went and asked about a caravan that they could join. Due to the many robbers it was too dangerous to travel onwards alone.

"The next caravan is expected from Tyre early the day after tomorrow," he told Mary. "But Jekamiah, the village potter, has offered us to stay with him until then. That gives you a chance to take a day of rest before we have to move on."

Mary gratefully let Joseph lead her to Jekamiah's house. Naamah, his wife, smiled at her and refreshed her and Joseph with a cup of cool water. With it she served small tarts made from dried figs. When Mary shyly offered her help in preparing the evening meal, Naamah smiled and declined, saying, "You better rest; this journey will be strenuous enough for you."

The caravan already arrived the next evening, shortly before it got dark, and camped at the outskirts of the village. Joseph left Mary under Naamah's care and went to meet the leader of the caravan. Uzziel, hardly older than Joseph, agreed to take the young couple along.

Very early in the morning, just at dawn, they started to leave. They first went east to cross the Jordan because, as pious Jews, they did not want to go through Samaria. Before they reached the ford, an older woman stopped alongside Mary. "I'm Zibiah, Uzziel's mother. And you're Mary, aren't you?"

Mary nodded. "Yes, I'm Joseph's wife."

Zibiah looked at Mary's big abdomen. "How much longer?"

"About three weeks."

"Why do you have to take on such a long journey so late?"

"Because of the census. I assume you've heard of it?"

"Yes, I have. There are some others in the caravan who are traveling because of it. Are you originally from Jerusalem?"

"No, we have to go on to Bethlehem. My husband and I are both descendants of David."

"So it's Bethlehem! In the mountains of Judea. Well, luckily it's not very far from Jerusalem. But altogether it's quite a long journey for you. You know what? Uzziel gave me a donkey, so that I can ride if walking gets too strenuous for me. I can easily share it with you. Then we can take turns riding."

Mary hardly knew how to thank her. She had already asked herself how she could keep up with the caravan throughout the days of travel. But if she could rest on the donkey once in a while she could probably make it.

Zibiah kept her word. She got her donkey, and the two women took turns riding while the other walked beside it. This way Mary was able to keep up with the others.

On the third day in the afternoon they reached Jericho. Uzziel decided to camp there during the night. "The ascent to Jerusalem is long and steep. We don't really have time to manage this with the daylight left," he explained to the people entrusted to him.

By the time they left the next morning he had purchased another donkey so that his mother and also Mary, the only pregnant woman in the little caravan, could ride up the steep road. Joseph helped his wife to mount the animal, thanking Uzziel for his care. Jericho was situated more than one thousand feet below sea level. Up to the Mount of Olives, behind which the destination of the caravan was located, they had to master more than 3,300 feet of height difference through a desolate, dusty chalk desert.

They needed several hours for their ascent. The last drop out of the water skins had been sucked out, the lips felt rough and cracked, the dust had gone through all their clothes and together with the sweat had built an uncomfortable crust on the skin. Breathing became more difficult; the dry dust made them cough more and more. Would they ever make it to the top?

And then it was just a few more steps, and they stood at the edge of the Mount of Olives. Nobody talked, they were so overwhelmed by the sight. Even those who had seen it before, maybe even many times were silent. In front of them the city of Jerusalem lay in all her splendor, surrounded on all sides by the protecting hillsides.

They remained speechless for quite a while. Then someone began to sing Psalm 125, and one by one all the others joined in:
> Those who trust in the LORD are like Mount Zion,
> Which cannot be shaken but endures forever.
> As the mountains surround Jerusalem,
> So the LORD surrounds his people
> Both now and forevermore...[1]

Slowly the caravan wound its way down the Mount of Olives to the city gate.

---

[1] according to TNIV

2: Shobana
Lonach, Sri Lanka – ca. 2006

"I don't like it!" With an angry frown on his face, the father looked at the mother. "I don't want our kids to go to those Christians with their strange school."

"Oh, please!" Eight-year-old Arumugam (ah-ROO-moo-gahm) looked up at his father. "It's so nice there!"

"Yes, it is!" Seeta, his older sister, nodded affirmatively. Six-year-old Shobana (SHOH-bah-nah) didn't dare to speak up. She only looked at her father imploringly.

"One day the gods will punish us for this," the father grumbled. Then he hastened away to his work on the tea plantation. Lots of weeds needed to be removed.

Silently Shobana watched her mother rub her legs with soap and salt as a protection against the leeches that swarmed over the tea plantations in damp weather. Then the mother swung the large green sack over her shoulder, laid the loose end of her sari over her head and grabbed the small packet with the rotis. These flat round loaves of bread were made from whole wheat flour and ground coconut and baked on both sides. One of these she would eat for breakfast on the tea plantation a little later, the other for lunch. Then she opened the wooden door of her small house and stepped outside into the cool, damp morning. With the other women she went to pick tea leaves, as she had done almost every day of her adult life. All the mountains, not only around Lonach, but for miles and miles in every direction, shone in the strong green of the vast tea fields, among which the colorful saris of the tea pickers shone like scattered flowers.

Shobana, whose name "beauty" suited her well, shivered in the cold air coming in through the door when her mother left. She stepped over to the little fire where her mother had baked the rotis for her day on the plantation. But Seeta, named for the wife of the Hindu god Ram, took their three-year-old little brother Sivalingam (see-vah-LING-gahm) by the hand and told Shobana, "Come, it's time; we need to go."

The earth felt cold and soft beneath their bare feet. Arumugam, Shobana and Seeta with Sivalingam hurried along between the two rows of houses. The plantation owners had had them built with blocks of concrete, sealed with mud and covered by a corrugated metal roof. A wooden door protected the small living room and tiny bedroom from snakes, leopards and other animals. A single window let in some light. It could be closed by a wooden shutter.

The cold wind gave them a final push as the four children entered the room which the Christians from Hatton had rented. They breathed a sigh of relief as they sat down, legs crossed, with several other children from the village. Then they all gratefully received the small bowls filled with milk and boiled grains.

But before they could eat they all bowed their heads. The man who had distributed the food closed his eyes. He thanked his Christian God, whom he called Jesus, for the nourishing meal. Only then the children were allowed to fill their empty stomachs.

The name Jesus reminded Shobana of the film she had seen with the other villagers a long time ago, as it seemed to her. Actually it had only been about two years, but the six-year-old couldn't think in such time frames, especially as the seasons this close to the equator didn't really help with calculating. But she still remembered that this man Jesus had healed many sick people and had taken little children into his arms. After that scene she had fallen asleep in her mother's arms. But the Christians talked a great deal about Jesus and addressed him as if he was standing right beside them, although nobody could be seen.

After breakfast little Sivalingam stayed for day care while Seeta, Arumugam and Shobana walked to school together with the other village children. A school for several villages had been built on a mountain in the middle. The students from Lonach had to climb up a path between the tea bushes.

They had almost reached the school when Arjun (ar-YOON), one of the older boys from the next village, came running towards them. He was waving his hands madly in the air and screamed, "Quick! Run away! Hurry! Hurry!"

Immediately everybody turned and tore down the mountain, Arjun close behind. What terror might be chasing them? A poisonous snake? A wild boar? Or maybe even a leopard, driven out of the jungle by hunger?

Down in the village they fled to the community hall, shoved each other in, and slammed the door shut. Still gasping for breath they turned to Arjun and looked at him inquiringly.

"Hornets!" Arjun panted. "A whole swarm. Somebody disturbed their nest. Several of us got stung."

"Oh no!" Arumugam exclaimed. "What now? Are they dead?" Shobana grabbed Seeta's hand and clung to her.

"I don't know," Arjun confessed. "But I certainly won't go up there again today." He opened the door a little and peered through the gap.

"Me neither! Me neither!" several others agreed. After a while they found the courage to step out of the building. There they nervously huddled in front of the door and stared up the path. Surely the hornets wouldn't come down here!

Suddenly Shobana remembered her father's final words before he left the house that morning. "One day the gods will punish us for that." Was this already the punishment of the angry gods? Trembling she turned to Seeta to ask her about it.

Before her sister could answer, Arumugam shrieked, "There! They're coming!"

"Who? What? The hornets?" Terrified cries came from all sides. But then they saw two students from Arjun's village running down the path towards them.

They had hardly arrived when they were surrounded and questioned. "Yes," they confirmed, "several got stung.

The teacher took them down to the doctor, and the school is closed for today."

While the family was eating their evening meal of rice, dhal and curry, Seeta and Arumugam stole frequent glances towards their father. Had he heard about the hornet attack? And would he forbid them to go to the Christian Sunday School tonight? They fervently hoped he wouldn't. This evening they meant to practice more of the dances for the Christmas program in the Christian center in Hatton in a few weeks. They had to go. They were needed.

Only Shobana didn't look up. Her father's warning was constantly circling in her mind. What if something even worse happened?

Fortunately the father didn't say anything about the incident. After the meal Seeta and Arumugam rushed to the Sunday School. Shobana followed reluctantly. She didn't join in the singing at the beginning, although that was the part she loved most.

Before they split into three age groups, Seeta told the pastor about the hornet attack that morning. "My father says the gods will punish us because we go to the Christians. Is that true?"

Shobana caught her breath. What would the pastor answer to that?

He responded with another question. "Why are we learning those dances?"

"Because we want to perform them at the Christmas program in Hatton," Shanti, who sat beside Seeta, replied.

"And what do we celebrate at Christmas?"

Arumugam knew that. "The birth of Jesus."

"Who is Jesus?"

"A son of God," Sundar (SOON-dar) shouted from the back row.

"Not *a* son of God," corrected the pastor, "but *the* son of God. Jesus is the only son of the only true God. He came into the world as a little baby, grew up and became a man to help us, not to hurt us. He loves us so much that we cannot even imagine it. And he is mightier than anything else in the whole world; mightier than the hornets, mightier than all other gods, mightier than all evil spirits."

Shobana took a very deep breath. Jesus was mightier than Ram and all the other gods? Then she didn't need to fear those angry gods anymore. How wonderful that Jesus came into the world!

3: Ulrike
Lüneburg[2], Germany – ca. 1975

"Oh, look, Ines! Isn't that one beautiful?" Ulrike (ool-REE-kah) pointed at a Barbie doll in the shop window and then put her arm through her friend's. "I'd love to get that as a Christmas present."

"Well, you can write it on your wish list. Or don't you have one?"

"Oh yes, I do. When I get home I'll write it down immediately."

"Would you like to know what I'd like to get?" Ines (EE-nihs) lowered her voice and made a mysterious face.

"No, you haven't told me yet. What is it?" Ulrike also spoke more quietly as if the people rushing by behind their backs were not allowed to hear it.

"Come; I'll show you." Ines turned from the shop window. Obviously her big wish was not sold at the toy shop. Arm in arm the two girls pushed through the pre-Christmas crowd. Above them, large bows of Christmas greenery with brightly shining stars were spanning the street. All shop windows were decorated festively. At some shops Christmas music spilled out onto the street the moment the doors were opened. From somewhere a delicious smell wafted towards them, so that Ulrike stopped and sniffed. "Mmm!"

But Ines went on and pulled Ulrike along with her. "How much farther is it?" Ulrike asked when they turned into a side street.

"Not much further!" Ines walked faster, and Ulrike tried to keep up with her. At last Ines stopped, and Ulrike curiously looked into the shop window. In the front a turtle was slowly crawling along in a wooden box. Behind it several budgerigars in different colors were hopping

---

[2] pronounced LOO-neh-boorg

around in a big cage. In a second box two white rabbits crouched, each in one corner. And over to one side an iguana was dozing in a glass-like box.

Ulrike looked from one animal to the other. "And which of these do you want? The purple budgie? I love that color!"

"Oh no! No bird! No, look into that corner!" Ines pulled her friend to one side and pointed at a little brown thing with dense fur. "That doggie there. Isn't it too cute? Look at the tiny nose tip! Like a little black button! And that look on its face! It's so cute! I've just got to have it!"

"What will your parents say to that?"

"I've already told my mother. She thinks it's a good idea. But she wants to talk to Papi[3] first. He'll agree, I'm sure. Because I'm so alone without any brothers and sisters. You're much better off!"

"Better??" Ulrike almost screamed. "You call that better? I could easily do without my brothers, and even Reni (RAY-nee) is getting more and more unbearable since she's able to walk. Now nothing's safe from her."

"Oh, but she's so cute! I wish I had such a little sister. Or a brother. I'm only alone all the time."

"Be glad! A little sister's bad enough, but younger brothers are just awful. And I have to endure two of that sort. You're lucky because you live in peace!"

Ines didn't contradict her although she thought differently about it. "Come; let's go home," she suggested. "I still have homework to do. I won't be able to finish it if I'm late."

The two girls turned away from the window and hurried back to the main shopping street. Silently they pushed through the crowd one after the other. Only when they had left the town center did Ines take her friend's arm again. "Are you angry, Ulrike?"

"No, no," Ulrike said although her face spoke a different language.

---

[3] German for Daddy, pronounced PAH-pee

Ines didn't press her any further, only clasped Ulrike's arm more tightly. She didn't want to start an argument now.

For a while they walked on silently. At a street corner Ulrike stopped. "Do you mind, Ines, to walk the last block alone? I want to look in on my Omi[4]."

"Um, no, I don't. Just go ahead. I don't have to walk much further anyway. Bye, Ulrike."

"Bye, Ines. See you tomorrow. And I hope for you that you'll get the little dog. It's really cute."

"Yes, isn't it?" Ines smiled happily as if she was already holding the little animal in her arms. Then she crossed the road and ran home.

Ulrike turned into a side street and hastened along the sidewalk. Her friend's words pierced her mind like needles. *How can she say something like that? She has no idea how annoying younger siblings are. And so many! One really would've been enough!*

At her grandmother's a warm light shone out of the living room window. This meant she was at home. Relieved, Ulrike pressed the bell.

Soon the door was opened. "Oh, Ulrike! What a lovely surprise! How nice! Come in quickly. It's cold outside."

Ulrike took off her coat and hung it up, on a hanger, the way her granny liked it. Then she followed her grandmother into the living room. "Mmm, what a wonderful smell!"

"Yes, yes." Granny laughed. "You came exactly at the right time. I just finished baking several sheets of cookies. Now I'll make some hot chocolate for you, and then you can test the cookies, one of each kind."

When she came back from the kitchen with the filled tray she put down a mug full of steaming hot chocolate in front of Ulrike and added a plate with the promised cookies. Then she lit two candles on the advent wreath on the table. "See, now we can make ourselves comfortable. Does Mami[5] know that you're here?"

---

[4] German for Granny, pronounced OH-mee
[5] German for Mommy, pronounced MAH-mee

"Well, not really. Ines and I went Christmas shopping. But Ines had to go home earlier than I did, so I thought I could drop by without Mommy getting worried. Besides ..." Ulrike stopped.

"What, 'besides?'"

Ulrike blushed and lowered her head. "Besides she has Benni and Fred and Reni now. She doesn't need me."

The grandmother looked searchingly at Ulrike for a while before she quietly asked, "Are you very sure about that?"

Shrugging her shoulders, Ulrike took a cookie. While she chewed on it without realizing how delicious it tasted she remembered what her mother had told her only this morning: "You're my big girl. I'm so glad to have you and that you're already such a big help." Hurriedly Ulrike took the mug and drank some chocolate, as if she could drown the memory of her mother's words.

For a while she stared at her plate. Then she sighed and whispered, "It just doesn't work."

"What doesn't work, Ulrike?" The grandmother sat down beside her and put an arm around her shoulders.

"What Jesus said. That we should love our brothers. It's impossible. He doesn't know how it feels if you have to put up with younger siblings."

"Are you sure he doesn't know?"

"How should he? He didn't have any. It says that he was God's only son."

"But he was not Mary's only son. He had several sisters with whom he grew up, and at least four brothers. Their names are mentioned in the Bible."

"So many? Well! Yes, but...they were always very obedient and always did what he told them to do."

"To the contrary. They made fun of him and said he was mad. Only after he had risen did they believe in him. Jesus knows very well how difficult it can be to live with siblings. He entered this world as a little baby and grew up like a normal child, so that he would know how children think and feel. He came to us and became like us, and *that* is exactly what we celebrate at Christmas."

4: Fahmida
Seeran Valley, Pakistan – 2005

Trembling, Fahmida cowered on a piece of broken wall and looked at her destroyed home. She pulled her shawl more tightly around her while tears again filled her eyes. By now two months had passed after the terrible earthquake that had brought so much suffering and death and devastation to Seeran valley in the north of Pakistan. Never would she forget that day in October: the swinging ground that opened up fissures everywhere, the dust and noise of collapsing houses, the cries of terror, of pain, and of desperation. Only a few seconds before her mother had sent her out of the house to get something for her. Then the ground knocked her down, and behind her the house caved in, burying her mother, tiny newborn brother and little two-year-old sister under it. None of them survived.

Fahmida didn't know how long she had lain there on the ground, motionless and almost paralyzed with horror. Alia (AH-lee-ah), her older sister, had found her there. Alia and Kamran, the oldest brother, were among the few that had survived the collapse of their school and had not been severely injured. But Ibrar, third among the siblings, had died under the rubble.

The rest of that day Fahmida had felt like she was in a fog. Sometime during the day she understood that her father was still alive but severely injured and that somebody was searching for her mother and younger siblings under the rubble that had been her home. Later Alia had brought her some water to drink. The steel water pipes that brought the fresh mountain water down from the mountains had not been destroyed.

They had spent the night in the open, all three of them pressed closely together to keep warm. The next morning while Kamran went on searching through the remains of their house, Alia took Fahmida along to see their father.

Alia gave him something to drink. Fahmida huddled down beside him and looked anxiously into his face contorted with pain.

During that day they had the first positive experience after the main earthquake the previous morning. A group of medical doctors arrived in Seeran valley from the far away country of Germany. They started to care for the injured, dressed Father's wounds, put his broken leg in a splint and arranged for him to be transported to the next hospital that was still operating and had not collapsed like the one in the valley had.

A few days later Pakistani soldiers had carried sugar, cookies and other dry food items into their valley. More helpers from foreign countries came and brought more food. They also brought used clothes and gave them to those people that had lost their own.

Fahmida's body shook when she relived all that. She looked across the valley up to the mountains on the other side of the Seeran River. Above the tree line the slopes rose bare, naked and steep. Her eyes wandered along the ridge up the valley. Far away the first snow glistened on the higher peaks. How would they survive the winter? It was already very cold. In a few weeks the snow would have reached the bottom of the valley. Without any shelter they would all freeze to death.

Around Fahmida most of the houses lay in ruins. The frames had been made from tree trunks, with big rocks from the fields in between, coated with clay, some of them built halfway into the rock face. Hardly any of these structures had withstood the earthquake. Where should the survivors go to live through the coming winter?

The sun appeared from behind a cloud and made the water of the Seeran River sparkle. Fahmida's eyes followed the windings of the river down to the collapsed bridge. Near the bridge a few goats that had survived the disaster were drinking from the now ice-cold water.

"Oh, here you are, Fahmida!" The girl jumped when suddenly the voice of her older sister sounded behind her. "Come!" Alia helped her up and protectively took her hand. "Some new trucks have arrived with more assistance."

Reluctantly Fahmida let herself be pulled down the road by her sister. As the trucks couldn't drive up to their village due to the destruction, the girls had to run quite a distance down the valley to pick up the packages. When at last they arrived, Fahmida saw Kamran standing with the other boys.

Several strangers stood in front of a truck. One of them looked like a Pakistani but was not wearing the familiar punjabi but modern clothing. The other three men obviously came from other countries. When she saw them, Fahmida hid behind Alia.

"Don't be silly," Alia quietly chided her. "They won't harm us. They only want to help us." But Fahmida wasn't so sure and only cautiously peeked out from behind Alia's back.

The stranger, who looked like a Pakistani, now started to speak to the people. He spoke Urdu, their country's language, so that they could understand him. "We're Christians," he explained. "We've heard about your emergency. I'm from Lahore, and these my friends here came from very far away, from a country called Germany. They want to help you get safely through the coming winter, so they've brought winter-proof tents and warm blankets for you. And they promised to come again and bring more help. Next year they want to rebuild your school."

Suddenly Fahmida pricked up her ears. For now she heard Kamran's voice: "You're Christians; we're not. Why are you doing all this for us?"

"This month we celebrate the birth of God's Son Jesus Christ," the Pakistani stranger explained. "God gave us his son to help us because he loves us so much. We want to pass on this love to other people and want to help them. We do this because of Jesus, God's free gift to us."

5: Filipe
Lisbon, Portugal – 1978

Clutching the balustrade with both hands, Filipe stood at the scenic overlook Nossa Senhora do Monte. Silently the seventeen-year-old looked down onto the houses of Lisbon and the leisurely flowing waters of the Tejo River. Now and then he heaved a sigh. Only one more week until Christmas! At home that had always been such a warm, happy family celebration. But now everything was empty inside him, and he was in no mood for celebrating. He was all alone – alone in the country of his ancestors. This morning he had set foot in it for the first time. Before he had only known it from his grandmother's tales.

She and his grandfather had emigrated from here to Africa as a young couple, to the Portuguese colony of Mozambique. In the south of the country near the capital, they had cultivated some land and built up a farm. Their oldest son José, Filipe's father, had taken over the farm after the grandfather had died. Filipe and his little sister Marisa had been born there.

They had done well on the farm. And after the Church of the Nazarene had planted a new congregation near their place, they had found their spiritual home there and enjoyed the fellowship with the other believers. Only the death of his grandmother had cast a shadow over them for a while.

Then one day they had received disturbing news. The natives had risen up against the white conquerors, and the fighting drew nearer and nearer. And then the horrible day came when his father was killed.

"Go, Filipe, and hide yourself before they also kill you," his mother urged him. He was twelve years old at the time. "Try to fight your way through to the south and cross that border. And when you're able, go back to our old homeland!"

"To Portugal? Alone? What about you? And Marisa?"

"Yes, yes, to Portugal! And you need to go alone. One can hide himself better than three. I'll try to go there as well with Marisa. But now go before it's too late! May God protect you, my boy!"

Filipe sighed inwardly when he remembered that. *I wish I knew what happened to Mama and Marisa. If only they didn't also get killed like Daddy and so many other people! Oh, I just hope they managed to leave Mozambique! Maybe they're actually here in Lisbon. But if they are, where could they be? And how am I to find them in this huge city?*

The days and weeks of his flight from Mozambique into South Africa via the southern border – no, he didn't even want to think about that. After wandering around for a long time he had found a new place to stay on the farm of a Dutch family. It took him a while to recover from the deprivation of his long wanderings. But then he threw himself into the work on the farm with all the energy he had left. For his efforts he got free food and lodging and a little money on the side. With iron discipline he had saved everything, until after some years he thought to have collected enough to start his long journey home.

In Durban, the most important harbor of South Africa, he went on board. The captain allowed him to do some small services to get a lower fare so that he could keep a little money for starting new in his unknown homeland.

And now he was standing here looking down on the city of his forefathers. After his arrival early in the morning he had wandered back and forth through the city, not knowing where to go. He had noticed how shabby some of the houses looked in the narrow and steep roads of the old part of town. But he also saw the cleanliness of the city, the beauty of the magnificent churches and many other buildings. The numerous tiles had especially caught his eye. Some of them adorned whole house fronts. Several were very colorful, but quite a few were in pretty, blue-and-white patterns and even huge spread-out pictures. The Tower of Belém he had seen only from a distance. But he had recognized it, as his grandmother had had a picture of it in her room.

For a while the setting December sun bathed Castelo de São Jorge in a warm reddish shimmer. Then dusk began to settle on the city. Everywhere lights were blazing up. Filipe again sighed deeply. Then he started to pray. He asked God to lead him to a Church of the Nazarene if there was one in town. "And, please, if possible, let me find my mother and Marisa if they're still alive!"

He turned around, his shoulders drooping, and walked down into the lower part of Lisbon. In the Rua Aurea he suddenly stopped. What was that? Over the noise of the traffic he heard some singing. That sounded like a Christmas carol! Curiously he went on to find the spot where the tune was coming from.

A few steps ahead there was an opening between the houses, like a small plaza. At the end of this plaza rose an elaborate, lighted elevator with six levels which was obviously for transporting pedestrians up to the upper town. On the stairs at the foot of it a group of young people were cheerfully singing one Christmas carol after the other.

Filipe listened with rapt attention. Suddenly he discovered a dark-skinned boy among the young people. Carefully he worked his way through the other listeners until he stood near him. After the last carol the young people mixed with the crowd and distributed invitations to their services.

Hurriedly Filipe stepped up to the dark-skinned boy. "Are you from Africa?" And when the boy nodded, he continued, "From where in Africa?"

"From the Cape Verde Islands. Why do you ask?"

"I was born and grew up in Mozambique. But because of the uprising we had to flee. Where we lived my family belonged to the Church of the Nazarene, and I had hoped ..."

"To the Church of the Nazarene?" The boy's eyes began to sparkle. With a wide smile he extended his hand to Filipe. "My name's Marcos, and my friends and I belong to the Lisbon First Church of the Nazarene. You're very welcome to join us!" Excitedly he then explained the way to the church and pressed one of the invitations into Filipe's hand.

Expectantly but also a little shyly, Filipe entered the church building for the Sunday service the next morning. Marcos waited in the foyer to meet him, welcomed him and led him to one of the front rows. But before he could seat himself a loud cry split the air. "Filipe! Filipe! O my Filipe!" With arms wide open, a woman rushed up to him, followed by a fourteen-year-old girl.

"Mama, oh, Mama!" he stammered, unable to move. The next moment his mother threw her arms around him, sobbing for joy, while the girl clasped his hand.

Could it be true? Or was he dreaming? But hadn't he prayed about this yesterday? God had answered his prayer, and very quickly! He had found his mother again! And his sister as well! What an immense joy! What a wonderful gift! A Christmas present! Now he would be able to really celebrate Christmas the next weekend. With his own family! "Thank you, Lord, my God," he whispered. "Thank you! Thank you!"

6: Kendrick
Vancouver, Canada – 2013

"Mommy[6], when will they finally arrive?" Five-year-old Kendrick stomped his foot. He was standing at the living room window, looking out. The bay window gave him the possibility of seeing in both directions along the road.

"Well, you need a little more patience, Kenny." His mother looked at the clock and calculated. "Daddy wanted to meet Aunt Betty in Merritt at ten. They can't be back before one."

"Why didn't Aunt Betty just come here?"

"Because she had to get back to Kelowna. Uncle Colin still needs to work on Monday, and Aunt Betty as well. They'll join us on the 24th so that we can celebrate Christmas and Boxing Day together as we always do."

"But why are Kathlyn, Roslyn and...and Madlyn already coming today?"

The mother smiled. "Because we've planned something special with all of you tonight, since the weather forecast has at last predicted two days without rain."

"Something special?" Kendrick turned around. "What's that?"

"I won't tell." She put a hand on his shoulder and planted a quick kiss on his cheek. "Let's keep it a surprise. But now I need to prepare lunch; they could be here in about half an hour. And you know your big brother is always ravenously hungry."

"Matthew?"

"Of course; who else? You just have one brother!"

Kendrick muttered something unintelligible and turned back to the window.

---

[6] American version that is also used in parts of Canada

At a quarter past one his father's SUV stopped in front of the garage. In an instant the house was full of laughter and chatter. The three cousins from the mountains weren't of the quiet kind. The fact that they had been allowed to come a few days early without their parents had been a special treat to excite them. The mysterious announcement for the evening added to their excitement.

"I've seen Santa Claus!" Kendrick tried to get their attention. "He even talked to me and ..." He broke off when his mother put her finger to her mouth and at the same time he got kicked by Matthew under the table.

"Didn't tell anything!" he mumbled. The girls hadn't even paid attention to him. But he had almost given away the secret that yesterday he had been to the mall with Mommy and Matthew where they had bought three pretty scarves for the cousins. The mother wanted to put them into the girls' Christmas stockings that would be hung up by the fireplace with those of her sons the evening before Christmas. According to the tradition, Santa Claus would come during the night with his sleigh and the reindeer to fill them with delicious things like chocolate bells, nuts, cookies, candy sticks, and other sweets. But Kendrick already knew that his parents would be the ones to add some practical things like nice pens, toothbrushes, pocket-sized Kleenex packages, and similar stuff and also a small special gift. Last year he had received a few small toy cars and Matthew even a music CD.

While the mother then had bought a few small things for her sons' stockings, Kendrick had been allowed to stand beside the huge decorated Christmas tree and beside Santa Claus. Matthew stayed with him and kept the small hand in his bigger one. Their mother knew she could rely on her ten-year-old.

Dusk had not even begun when all seven of them got into the car in the afternoon. Matthew pulled Kendrick with him into the far back onto the additional seats put in by his father so that their guests could have the three seats on the regular rear bench. In the front yards along the road lots of decorations made up of many lights were shining: Santa Claus figures, stars, Christmas trees, many different animals, and other things. When the car turned around the first corner Kendrick saw a big sleigh with nine reindeers in front of the sleigh and in it Santa Claus with several parcels–all made out of lights. Kendrick knew that his voice could not get through against three chattering girls to ask his parents. So he tugged at Matthew's arm, pointed at the reindeer team of lights and shouted, "Which of those is Rudolph?"

Matthew grinned. "The leading one, of course! The first one in the front with the red nose; that's the leader!"

"I see!" Kendrick turned around and stretched his neck to get another look at that important animal. But it was already too far behind to be distinguished from the others. So he looked out the side window at all the other lighted figures, strings of lights on the guttering, around windows and doors, strung through trees and many more. Then suddenly he thought of something, and he pulled his brother's sleeve. "Why are Mary and Joseph not there? Daddy told us we celebrate Christmas because the Christ child was born."

Matthew shrugged his shoulders. "No idea! Maybe the people don't know that."

By now they had reached the highway and for a short while the father could drive faster. They had hardly crossed the Fraser River when the traffic became denser, and he had to slow down. Already before they reached the bridge to North Vancouver, they stood in a traffic jam for several minutes. The rest of the way to Panorama Park was stop and go, and when they reached the parking lot of the park it was already filled up so that they had to search for a while. At last they found a small place in one of the sidestreets. "Kenny, take my hand and stay with me," his father told him after they had left the car. "And you others link arms and take care to stay together and not lose each other in this crowd!"

"Why did we come here?" Kathlyn und Roslyn asked at the same time.

"To watch the Carolship Parade of Lights."

"What's that?" Madlyn wanted to know.

"You'll soon see. But first we need to walk there as we didn't get a closer parking spot. Be careful to stay together", he again admonished. He took a strong hold on Kendrick's hand and led the way, the others close behind. They had to walk several hundred yards through the now dark streets. Even from afar they could hear music, and the nearer they got to the park the stronger the smell of food became.

"Daddy, I want some French fries," Kendrick begged after they had reached the first booths. His father turned around. "What do you think, Peggy?"

His wife shrugged her shoulders. "Let all of them have some, or we won't have any peace."

Only after all five of the kids had eaten their fries and had their hands free again, did they try to get nearer to the shore. But they were stopped by an exclamation from Roslyn. "Face painting! Oh, may we?"

Although the father sighed he gave in. "Yes, but only if it's fast enough. We certainly don't want to miss the parade."

As there were several other kids waiting in line, there was just enough time left to have the girls' faces painted. Matthew didn't want any of it, but Kendrick pouted at first. But his father appeesed him by lifting him up on his shoulders. Then they hurriedly pushed through the crowd until they found a spot in the north of the park where they could see across the water.

It wasn't one moment too soon. The leading ship had already passed that spot but could still be seen well. One ship after the other glided past them. Each of them was adorned with numerous lights in many different colors that were mirrored in the dark water. The sight was so breathtakingly beautiful that in the beginning even the girls kept quiet. About a dozen illuminated ships had already gone past them before they found their voices once more. They started shouting to each other what they noticed, to be heard above the noise from the park behind them. "Look at that one; everything's pink!"

"And there's a big one with lights all around and on several levels!"

"Oh, look at that sailboat over there! Looks like a lighted Christmas tree!"

"Yes, and there're many sailboats all coming together, and they look like lots of pointed pyramids!"

Kendrick had watched the parade for quite a while, fascinated and silent. Then suddenly he bent down to his father's ear. "Daddy, why do they all have so many lights?"

"Well, you see, it's because of Christmas. The light points to Jesus. He said about himself that he is the light of the world. That's why we light so many candles at Christmas. You remember why we celebrate Christmas, don't you?"

"Yes, that's when Jesus came down to the earth." With new interest Kendrick followed the rest of the parade. It took a long time until the more than seventy decorated ships had glided past them. So it was already quite late before they were back in the car.

Kathlyn summarized what they all thought. "That was marvelous! Thank you so much, Uncle Gordon!"

7: Gergana
Sofia, Bulgaria – ca. 1998

Slowly the car bumped along the rough roads of Sofia, the capital of Bulgaria. Laura gazed intently out of the window. The wind seemed to be gaining speed. In the yards the branches of the trees swung faster and more fiercely. A moment later Laura cried, "It's snowing! Mommy, Daddy, look! It's snowing!"

It was true. At first only a few snowflakes were gliding down, but very quickly their number grew to hundreds and thousands. Soon there were so many snowflakes dancing in the air that Laura could hardly see the apartment buildings along the road.

"That looks like a snowstorm," her father murmured, and turned on the windshield wipers. "I'm glad it's not too much further." By now the snowflakes were swirling against the car almost horizontally, forcing him to slow down, so that they needed more than half an hour before they finally reached the orphanage.

Instantly the front door flew open and children came rushing out. Before Laura could even get out of the car the children had surrounded her parents, jumping and shouting and rejoicing. The smaller ones clung to the visitors' arms so that the older ones wouldn't push them away. Laura's parents laughed and hugged them and greeted everyone cheerfully.

Laura, who had never before accompanied her parents to the orphanage, was watching them with amazement. Immediately she realized how poorly these children were dressed. Nothing fit together, they had neither coats nor jackets, and most children didn't wear any shoes. Laura looked down at her warm winter coat and padded boots, and she shivered.

Suddenly she noticed a little girl standing apart from the cheerful crowd, looking longingly at the visitors. Laura slid down from her car seat and stepped towards her. "What's your name? How old are you?"

With big brown eyes the girl looked at Laura, but didn't answer. One of the older girls turned around and scoffed, "That's Gergana. She's seven, and she talks only when she wants to."

A little flustered Laura stared at Gergana (gehr-GAH-nah) and stammered, "I...I'm seven, too. How long have you lived here? Very long?"

Silently Gergana looked at Laura. Then she shook her head slowly.

The orphanage director sent the children back into the house and invited the missionary family into her office for a cup of coffee. Laura swung her feet back and forth while the adults were talking. She wanted to go and join the children. Gergana would not leave her thoughts.

At last they were led into the gym where the celebration was going to take place. All the children were seated and waiting for their guests. At the front of the little hall stood a bedraggled Christmas tree and a table covered in red and white paper, both covered in homemade decorations. The table was laden with candy, snacks and other sweet things. Behind them, the parcels which Laura's parents had brought were piled up. A few days earlier Laura had watched from a window as a truck pulled up beside their house and delivered the packages. While her mother was wrapping them in beautiful Christmas paper she told Laura that people from a faraway country had sent them for the poor in Bulgaria.

Laura pulled on her mother's sleeve, pointed at the candy and other sweets, and whispered, "Did all of that also come from very far away?"

"No," her mother whispered back. "That was donated by local businesses. But be quiet now; the program is starting."

The children had prepared a program of skits, songs and comedy. Each grade level performed their own piece, and some of the songs had even been written by the children. Then the door opened and...

"Father Christmas!" the children whispered.

But Laura quickly covered her mouth with her hand because she had almost shouted out loud, "Daddy!" At home she had seen her father try on the red coat with the white fur collar, and she knew exactly who was hiding under that coat.

Behind Laura's father a woman appeared, dressed in white with white stars pinned to her dress. On her head she wore a white crown. "Mommy," Laura whispered, "Who's that?"

"It's Mother Frost," the mother answered. Then she rose, stepped to the front, and gave a short speech. She explained that the reason people give and receive gifts at Christmas is because of the gift God gave us when he sent the baby Jesus to earth.

After the speech the children formed a line and slowly walked by Father Christmas and Mother Frost. Father Christmas gave each child one of the parcels and some of the sweets. Then Mother Frost wished them a happy New Year.

Only the parcels Laura's parents had brought were wrapped. The children had to wait until all had received their gifts and returned to their seats. Then they eagerly ripped them open and happily examined what they found.

Suddenly Laura nudged her mother and pointed at Gergana. The little girl sat there and gazed at her parcel with shining eyes, but without opening it. The mother took Laura's hand and walked over to Gergana. Stooping down to the small girl she asked, "Would you like me to help you unpack?"

Slowly Gergana shook her head and whispered, "Oh, it's so beautiful! I've never seen anything so beautiful."

"But you must open it," Laura's mother urged gently. "There's something special for you inside."

With big, incredulous eyes the child looked up and asked, "You mean there's more?"

Laura watched with her mouth open as Gergana slowly and carefully unwrapped the gift and peeked into the box, speechless with amazement. Only after additional encouragement from Laura's mother dared she take the blue rabbit out of the box. "Is this really mine?" she asked repeatedly before she cradled the stuffed animal in her little arms.

On the way home Laura asked her mother why the orphan girl had reacted so strangely.

"You see, poor little Gergana has never in her whole life received a gift or even seen a wrapped gift. So she mistook the wrapping for the present."

"But the real thing is inside," Laura objected. "That's the most important and most beautiful part. The wrapping's just the outside."

For a moment the mother was silent. Then she said, "Look, Laura, that's exactly what most people do with Christmas. They just see the outside, the beautiful wrapping. And they do not understand that the contents are the real thing: God coming to us as a tiny baby. That is the real Christmas."

This story is based on a true incident.

8: Pedro
Ecuador – ca. 2003

"Where ya drivin' to?"

Hernando squinted down at the boy who had suddenly appeared beside his truck just when he had wanted to get in. It was still very early in the morning; the night had just given way to the young, fresh daylight, and Hernando wanted to get an early start in order to reach his destination before darkness. The boy might have been ten years old and looked a bit shabby. "Why do you ask?"

"'Cause, maybe, I'd come along."

"Where do you intend to go?"

"Not sure 'bout that." The boy shrugged his shoulders. Then he blurted out, "Someplace what's far away from Guayaquil. I'm fed up wi' this city."

Hernando grinned. "Why's that?"

"Oh, 'cause this 'n' that! The worst is them cucarachas[7]. There's a downpour, an' all's covered, not jest wi' water but those 'orrible beasts. A body can't e'en find a decent place t' sleep."

"Place to sleep? Don't you have a home?"

The boy hung his head, shuffled his feet and mumbled, "No more."

"Don't you have any parents?"

He only shook his head.

"Any other relatives? An uncle? Or an aunt?"

Another headshake.

"What's your name, by the way?"

"Pedro."

"And the last one?" Hernando had flinched a little but tried to hide it.

"Dunno. Don't matter."

---

[7] Big black cockroaches

"Maybe it matters to me!" Hernando thoughtfully looked down on the boy's bent head. Was he telling the truth? He didn't seem to have anyone to care for him.

"What do you intend to do once you get to 'someplace'?"

Pedro again shrugged his shoulders. Then he lifted his head and looked at Hernando with pain in his face. "Th' other street boys don't want me. They think me's not good enough for 'em."

"Not good enough? What do you mean with that?"

"Well, they steal an' such if they be hungry, an' they beat folks up. But...I can't do that."

Hernando felt pity. And not only that. Something about this boy touched his innermost self. He opened the driver's door. "Go! Hop in and slide through. We can talk more on the way. I want to reach the mountains before the next shower hits."

As fast as a hare Pedro had jumped up the steps and climbed across the driver's seat onto the passenger's seat. Hernando swung himself after him, settled behind the steering wheel, closed the door and started the engine.

While the heavy truck struggled through the city of three million, the conversation between the two ceased. Hernando had to concentrate on his driving in the heavy traffic. He longed to get out of the hot humidity of the coastal plains into the much nicer climate of the Andes. And to get off the road before Christmas which was only a few days away.

Pedro slightly turned his head to look out of the corner of his eye at this man who had talked to him in such a friendly way, like nobody else had done for a long time. Could he trust him? Since his mother had died he had had nobody in whom he could confide. He didn't know anything about his father; his mother had never mentioned him.

But for the moment he vaguely answered all the questions Hernando asked him after they had escaped the chaotic traffic of the city. At the foot of the Western Cordilleras near the little town of Bucay they took a break.

Before Hernando shared his food with the boy, he bent his head and thanked God in his own words for his good care. Pedro stared at him. It reminded him of his mother who had also prayed before every meal although she had used a text she had learned by heart. The simple prayer and the generosity of the truck driver touched Pedro and swept away a good amount of his distrust.

When they traveled on up into the mountains Pedro intuitively started to open up; even he himself didn't know why he did it. A deeply hurt and neglected soul revealed himself to the man: a soul that feared the future and didn't know what to do or how to go on.

In Riobamba they reached the high valley between the two mountain ranges of the Andes, also called the "Avenue of the Volcanoes." Pedro pointed at a high mountain on their right where smoke was rising from the top. "Is that the Cotopaxi?"

"No, that's further north. But we'll also pass that one."

"That also smokin'?"

"Not just now. But nobody can tell when it'll start again. This one here, the Tungurahua, has been smoking like that for years. You'll see several other volcanoes before we reach Quito. And a little north of Quito runs the Equator that divides the world into north and south. That's why our country's called Ecuador. Did you know that?"

"Nope, I didn't."

"Do you know that in three days we'll have Christmas?"

"In three days?" Pedro swallowed hard and hung his head. "I plumb forgot."

In Ambato they took another break, and Hernando bought some food for himself and Pedro. While the boy chewed with his mouth full and obviously enjoyed the sumptuous meal, the man studied him closely. Only when Pedro declared himself totally satisfied did he turn the key in the ignition and pull the truck back onto the road. Right before darkness hit, they reached Quito at last.

Hernando drove the truck into the parking lot of the company for which he worked and turned off the engine.

Then he looked at the boy. "What do you intend to do now?"

Pedro shrugged his shoulders. "Dunno. Guess I'll look round a bit in town."

The driver regarded him searchingly for a moment. Then he quietly said, "Pedro, is your family name López?"

The boy flinched violently and stared at his benefactor. "How d'ya know?"

Hernando didn't answer but asked, "Was your mother's name Catalina?"

"Yes." Pedro's voice was barely audible. There was shock and fear in his eyes.

"And were you born on November 12, 1993, in Porotillo, a little bit north of Guayaquil?"

The boy's face had drained of all color. He nodded wordlessly. Then he hastily turned to the door. But the man grabbed his arm and cried, "Wait! Don't run away! Let me at least explain to you why I know all this."

Hesitantly Pedro turned back to him but didn't look at him. With his head bent, he waited for Hernando to go on.

"Listen, Pedro! My last name is also López. And I had a son, a baby, whose name was Pedro. But at that time I was without work, often drunk, and one day I left my wife and the baby because I just didn't know how to go on. I don't want to think about the years after that; they were just plain horrible. But around four years ago I met some people here in Quito who know God. Not just in theory, but they have a real relationship with him. They constantly talked about Jesus. It's a long story; maybe I can tell you later if you care to hear it. Two years ago I made peace with God, stopped drinking alcohol, and a few months later I got this job as a truck driver. And then I remembered my family. After a long search I had to face the sad news that my wife had died in the meantime. But nobody knew anything about my son. Since then I have prayed every day that I might find him." He cleared his throat loudly. "I believe today my prayers were answered."

While he talked Pedro's face had been lifting higher and higher. His eyes large and round, he now stared at him. "Is...this...true?"

"Yes, Pedro! You're my boy! In your face I've found similarity with your mother. And with me. I can hardly believe that at last I got you back! This is the most wonderful Christmas present I can ever think of! And now you'll come with me and stay with me, won't you? I'm very, very sorry that I abandoned you both years ago, and I want to ask your forgiveness."

Pedro intently looked at him. His eyes shone with tears, and he sniffed. He still hesitated a moment as if he had to contemplate what he had heard, to take it all in. Then he threw himself into the open arms. "Papá, my Papá!" was all he could squeeze past the lump in his throat. But the way he clung to his father said more than all the words in the world.

9: Eruera
Wanaka, New Zealand – ca. 2004

Eruera (eh-roo-EH-rah) woke up suddenly as something had startled him. What was that? It sounded as if somebody was sliding down the roof intending to make as much noise as possible. Then Eruera heard shrill giggles in the yard. He listened. More loud giggling. That could only be Keas, the audacious, curious, playful parrots that lived here in the mountains of the southern island of Aotea-roa (ah-oh-TEH-ah-ROH-ah), the land of the long white cloud, as the Maoris (mah-OH-rees) called New Zealand.

But it's summer now! Daddy said they love the cold and only come down here around July. So what are they doing in Wanaka in December? For a while longer Eruera listened to the giggling and rumbling outside his window; then he went back to sleep.

The next morning the whole family enjoyed a leisurely breakfast. It was only a few more days till Christmas, the school year was finished, six long weeks of vacation were before them, and even the father who taught at the local elementary school did not have to leave the house early in the morning. As a pakeha (pah-KEE-hah) – whiteskin – Stephen Sheridan had married a wahine (wah-HEE-neh), a Maori woman named Hinetitama (hih-ne-tee-TAH-mah). That's why all four of the children bore two names, a Maori one and an English one which resembled the Maori name in its meaning.

"You still didn't tell us where we'll go for vacation this time," Aoatea (ah-oh-ah-TEH-ah) Dawn asked her parents. Being fourteen, she was the oldest of the four siblings.

"Oh my, didn't we?" A spark of fun danced in her father's eyes. "We thought for this year it might be a good idea to..." He stopped, looking at them roguishly. "... to stay home."

Immediately a storm of protest arose from the three older children. Only Anahira (ah-nah-HEE-rah) Angela, the three-year-old, first looked from one to the other in confusion, then joined in.

"Daddy, you're just making fun of us; we don't believe that," Aoatea exclaimed after the shouting had died down.

Airini (ah-ee-REE-nee) Irena, only one year younger, cut in before the father could even open his mouth. "I want to go to Rotorua[8] on North Island where there are geysers and hot springs. We talked about that at school. They said it's wonderful to bathe in them."

"Oh no!" Aoatea rejected the idea vehemently. "There are also lots of sulphur springs; they stink horribly, like rotten eggs." She shuddered violently to emphasize her words.

"Then let's go to Tongariro[9] National Park..."

"Help me, no!" Aoatea lifted both hands cutting her sister short. "Do you want to be buried by ash? It's only a few years ago that all three of those volcanoes erupted for the umpteenth time; you were already born. They scattered lots of ash across half of North Island. No, thank you. I don't need something like that!"

"Nothing suits you. Do you by any chance have a better suggestion?" Airini threw her oldest sister an angry look.

"I certainly do! I would love to go to the seaside and see the Pohutakawa[10] trees in full bloom. They say everything glows bright red, and it's..."

"Looking at trees! What a silly thing!" Airini's voice was full of contempt.

Eight-year-old Eruera Edward hurriedly stuffed the rest of his breakfast into his mouth and quietly left the room without anybody noticing. Let his two older sisters fight each other. That way he had some peace for a change. He felt so sick of their constant attempts to mother him. And his wish to go down to the Fjordland National Park in the

---

[8] pronounced row-toh-ROOH-ah
[9] pronounced TAHN-gah-REE-roh
[10] pronounced puh-HOO-tah-KAH-wah

southwest of their own island? He was sure they would both strongly reject that suggestion.

Curiously Eruera strolled into the yard. He wanted to find out what the nightly noise had meant. Could it really have been Keas? In the warm summer sunshine it seemed pretty unlikely.

In the middle of the yard he found Anahira's doll Reka (reh-KAH). The little girl obviously had forgotten it in the yard yesterday. But how that poor doll did look! The pretty dress was hanging down in shreds, and the eyes were two empty holes. Where had those pretty brown eyes with the long lashes gone? Eruera carefully picked up the doll and realized that one arm and both legs had been torn off. The little body was covered with dents and holes. Had the Keas worked on the doll with their sharp beaks?

Eruera stared at the battered doll. *What will Anahira say to that? Surely she'll cry bitterly and be really sad.* But Eruera wanted to avoid that. He dearly loved this little sister. *What can I do? Is there a chance at all to save it?*

Suddenly an idea popped into his mind. Hastily he collected all the parts together, shoved them under his T-shirt, and sneaked out of the yard without telling anybody. Ten minutes later he rang the bell at the parsonage. Mrs. Parker, the pastor's wife, opened the door. She kindly welcomed him and took him into the house. In the hallway he pulled the doll's pieces out from under his shirt and explained why Reka was so horribly torn. "Is it possible to repair the doll? And maybe make a new dress? I still have a few dollars; I'll gladly give them for that."

"That's very kind of you, Edward. Come along into the office where my husband is working. We want to look closely at this mess and figure out what we can do. I myself don't have much time this close to Christmas. But I'm sure my mother will help sew a new dress. Come!"

Half an hour later Eruera ran homeward whistling. On his right hand Lake Wanaka shone in the morning sun. Behind it Mount Aspiring rose, the mountain after which the national park here was named. White sailing boats were gliding across the water. Above the boy some hanggliders were floating through the air while he passed some hiking tourists. He didn't notice them. In his thoughts he was still with the Parkers. He had known that they wouldn't refuse to help him. How lovingly the couple did care for their little congregation! The day after tomorrow, which was Christmas Eve, he was supposed to come back. By then they hoped to have repaired most of the damage.

When he entered his home his father met him at the door. "What were you thinking to just run away without telling anybody? Where have you been? Your mother was really worried about you!"

Eruera's joy collapsed like a balloon pricked by a needle. He hung his head and muttered, "I'm sorry!"

"As a punishment you won't get any of the plum pudding on Christmas Day so you learn not to just run away when you want to. Now go to Mummy[11] and apologize!"

"Yes, Daddy." Eruera slowly dragged his feet into the kitchen. That was a very hard punishment. They only had plum pudding for Christmas, and he loved it. But he didn't want to say anything about the ruined doll.

Two days later Eruera sat in his room and wondered whether he should ask his mother or his father for permission to go so that he could pick up the hopefully repaired doll. He felt the need to give it to his little sister before Christmas so that she could stop being so sad. She had already cried for her doll several times, but up till now had always let herself be distracted.

While he was still contemplating this the doorbell rang. A little later his mother called him. Beside her stood Mrs. Parker, and on the table lay a big parcel. "I was going this direction anyway," the pastor's wife explained after she had greeted him. "So I thought I'd save you the trouble of coming to us."

After she had left, Hinetitama embraced her son. "Now I know where you were the other day. Mrs. Parker told me

---

[11] British version

everything. That was very kind of you to care for your little sister like that. And, of course, you'll get your part of the plum pudding tomorrow. And an extra-large piece of the turkey. But, in the future, you'll tell me when you have to go somewhere, won't you?"

"Yes, Mummy, I'll certainly do that!" Eruera nodded. Then he peered into the parcel. The doll did not look exactly like the other one. No dents or holes. The eyes were blue instead of brown. Also the color of the dress was a little different. But the doll looked pretty similar to the old one.

"May I give it to Anahira myself, Mummy?"

"Yes, of course! You deserve that privilege, my boy!" She stroked his hair. And when his little sister, with shining eyes, clasped her Reka in her arms Eruera's happiness was complete.

10: Sentwali
Massai-Amboseli, Kenya – ca. 1982

Taking long strides, Sentwali walked home. His naked feet darted almost noiselessly across the dry savanna. His eyes carefully scanned the ground in front of him. Only a few days ago a woman from his kraal (KRAHL) had been bitten by a black mamba and had died. These several-yard-long, thin snakes possessed very strong venom, and one could hardly be careful enough to avoid them.

The day had been hot. But now the sun had already sunk quite low. *Surely Njanu has already come home with the cattle and goats. I'd better hurry.* Soon darkness would cover the land. Twilight was short here in the southern part of Kenya, so near the equator.

Ahead of him, a little off to the right, two giraffes were walking across the plain in their strange swinging way. Not far from them a large herd of zebras passed by, probably on their way to one of the waterholes that the rainy season had filled so well that they had not dried out yet. Behind him Sentwali heard the faraway howling of hyenas. He hastened his steps.

The sun sank deeper and deeper. It was almost touching the horizon. Sentwali felt relief when he spotted the umbrella tree with the raw-hewn, backless benches under it. This was where the Massai who believed in Christ assembled for their services. And from here it was not far to his home kraal.

Just a little while later Sentwali ran through the opening in the massive thorny hedge that surrounded the Massai settlement. After he had passed, some women filled the opening with additional thorny branches for the night. These long, poisonous thorns kept wild animals out so that the Massai could sleep relatively protected in their low, flat huts made from cow dung. Their cattle, too, driven into the center of the kraal at night, were safe from the lions, leopards and hyenas. The cows were the Massai's main source of livelihood. Their main food source was cow's milk. Once in a while they mixed it with cow's blood, taken from the main artery of the animal. The wound was afterwards carefully closed with saliva, resin and soil. Only very rarely, for special occasions, they killed an ox to eat its meat.

Sentwali bent down to enter the hut through the low opening. Smoke was rising from the smoldering hearth that served also as the only source of light. Part of the smoke escaped out of a small hole in the ceiling, the rest floated along the ceiling and out through the door opening. Sentwali sat down on a three-legged stool. The seat was only a handbreadth above the ground. He breathed in the smell of the mash of cassava roots his mother had cooked. He could hardly wait for the evening meal to be served. It was the only meal of the day.

A little later, when he lay on his hard bed that was just raised a little above the ground, he couldn't go to sleep. Again and again he thought about what he had learned at the mission station this afternoon. Miss Taylor and Miss Miller, the two missionaries, had lived there for a long time telling the people about Jesus. Jesus was the only Son of the Creator-God who had created everything, even the majestic Kilimanjaro, whose top shone white almost the whole year, and, of course, the cows, goats and sheep with which the Massai made a living.

Very often Sentwali had heard about Jesus when the missionaries had talked about him, how he had healed the blind so that they could see again, had helped the lame so that they could walk again, how he had died a horrible death at two crossed wooden beams, but had come back to life again on the third day and returned to his Father-God.

But what he had not known before was how he had come down to earth to the people: that he had been born as a tiny helpless baby – like Sentwali's younger sister Hakima (hah-KEE-mah) and his little brother Maamuni (mah-MOO-nee) – and that he had to grow up like other children – as Sentwali himself who was now almost twelve years old; no, he hadn't known this. Today Miss Taylor had vividly told how God's son had to be born amidst the cattle, how he had been born and raised in poverty. And she had called the birth of Jesus a present, God's great gift to humans. She had also mentioned that the people in her far-away home country gave each other gifts once a year to commemorate this—around this time, when they celebrated the birth of God's son.

"I would like to do that as well," Sentwali mused. "I also would like to give a gift to somebody to remember the great gift of the Creator-God to us. But what could I give? And to whom?"

He brooded and brooded over this, but nothing came to his mind. It wasn't customary to give gifts in his tribe. Finally he fell asleep over it.

The next morning he and Njanu (in-JAH-noo), his younger brother by two years, drove the cattle out of the kraal as usual. With a sideways glance he noticed Mahiri (mah-HEE-ree), the son of his father's sister, playing with a small car made from wire. *Such a car I could make for Maamuni,* suddenly shot through his brain. *I'm sure my little brother would enjoy that. And my sisters? Kamilah's already grown up; she probably wouldn't want her younger brother to give her a gift. But Hakima! Yes, I could give her something. But what could that be? She'll hardly play with cars since she's a girl.*

After the two boys had watered the cattle at the next water hole they wandered slowly across the savanna and let the animals graze, carefully watching whether there was a wild animal sneaking up from somewhere.

At noon they spotted some vultures circling in the sky. Had a lion killed some prey and now the vultures were waiting for leftovers? To be on the safe side the two boys led their herd in the opposite direction.

On their way home the boys met several women and girls, Kamilah (kah-MEE-lah) among them, who were on their way to fetch water. With cool self-confidence they wore their wide stiff necklaces made from many colorful beads.

That would be something for Hakima, Sentwali thought. *She would surely enjoy some colorful beads and a little wire. Then she can make herself a pretty necklace.* Of course, Hakima wasn't yet allowed such splendid jewelry as Kamilah, who had already been circumcised and therefore was considered an adult. But thin, simple necklaces also adorned the necks of the younger girls.

Sentwali liked that idea. But how should he get wire and beads? The path across the hot, dusty savanna to the next town with a shop was long. And he had nothing that he could offer in exchange. He also didn't own one of those small, flat, round metal things the missionaries called coins.

After thinking hard for a long time he found a solution. *I'll walk to the mission station again tomorrow. The two women always have work to do where I can help. They always give me something for it, mostly something nice to eat. But this time I could ask for some beads and wire instead.*

The missionaries were never short of work, and they gratefully accepted Sentwali's offer. As they helped the Massai women to earn some money by selling their jewelry, they always had enough beads and wire in stock to pay Sentwali for his work. While he was still at the mission station Sentwali bent most of the wire into a car and hid it, so that Maamuni wouldn't see his gift too soon. But he made sure to leave enough for Hakima's necklace.

Never would Sentwali forget the shining eyes of his younger siblings when he gave them his gifts. Why, he hadn't known how much joy it brought to yourself to give joy to others. Had the Creator-God also been so joyful when he gave his son to the people?

11: Amol
Washim, India – 2003

With a frightened look in her eyes, Sumati (soo-MAH-tee) pressed the baby closer to her body as she hastened to follow her husband along the dusty road. In front of them an ox cart was plodding along. The tired young woman would have loved to sit down on the empty cart, but the two oxen were moving far too slowly. Prakash and Sumati hurried past them. They had to run if they wanted to save their child. The small, seven-month-old Amol (AH-mohl) was struggling harder and harder for each breath.

A rickety bus rushed past them, honking wildly. Quickly the young couple jumped to the side of the road. From experience they knew how recklessly most bus drivers steered their buses. A thick cloud of dust enveloped the little family. Sumati lifted the end of her sari and wrapped it around her child for protection. A moment later, loud ringing sent Prakash and Sumati to the roadside once more. A young man pedaled past them on his rickshaw, standing up so he could pedal faster.

I wish we could go on that rickshaw, Sumati thought. *How much easier and faster we could travel.* But they had no money for it. So they just tried to walk faster. When they had to make room for passing traffic they tried to avoid stepping in higher grass, as it often hid cobras, the most poisonous snake in India.

At last they reached the town of Washim and hurried to the new government hospital. But the doctor on duty only threw a brief glance at the gasping baby and sent them away: Nothing more could be done for the child.

Filled with despair, Prakash and Sumati staggered back to the road. Was there no help? Had they come too late? Would they lose their little treasure so soon? Or should they try seeing one of those new doctors who had opened their practices here after Washim became a district town?

No, that was impossible. The fees they charged were far too high. Prakash and Sumati were poor.

"We have to do something!" Sumati cried, almost beside herself with fear. "Look, he's already turning blue. Oh, who can help us?"

"Why don't you go to the Christians?" an old woman asked. She had heard Sumati's tortured cry.

"To the Christians?" Prakash looked at her in astonishment.

"Oh yes. Don't you know that they have a hospital here? For as long as I can remember. Look, you have to follow that road over there." The woman pointed in the right direction and explained the way.

"But we have no money," Prakash admitted.

"That's no problem. They'll help you anyway."

"Thank you!" As quickly as they could, the young parents pushed through the crowd. Out of breath they finally reached Reynold's Memorial Hospital, ran through the open gate, across the courtyard, and through the narrow passage beside the pharmacy into the inner court. A nurse who was standing there took one look at the bluish baby gasping for breath. She shouted, "Quick, get in there!" and pushed them into the consulting room.

"The child was born with a valvular heart defect," the doctor explained to the frightened parents after examining their child. "This has caused congestive cardiac failure. We'll do what we can. Maybe we can save him."

While the doctors immediately began the treatment, Prakash and Sumati dragged themselves out to the inner courtyard. They were so afraid of losing their precious baby boy that at first they didn't notice anything around them. But after some time they realized with astonishment that a group of nurses was decorating the hallways with colorful paper and lights in many colors. What did this mean?

In the evening they were allowed to see Amol for a few minutes. The little boy was sleeping in one of the many cribs in a nicely painted room. His complexion already looked much healthier.

Somewhat relieved Sumati joined several other women in the front courtyard of the hospital to light a fire on the ground and cook a meal for her husband and herself. They hadn't eaten the whole day and were now quite hungry.

The next morning they witnessed another strange thing. Almost all the doctors, the nurses, and even some relatives of patients assembled in a room full of benches. They sang songs about a God Prakash and Sumati had never heard about. Then a man got up and talked about a divine child named Jesus that was sent to the earth by his Father-God to help the people.

When one of the doctors asked this God to heal their little Amol, the young parents stared at him, surprised. That strange man was praying for their own child! And during the following days the parents repeatedly observed nurses stopping at Amol's crib to pray for his healing.

Every day Amol's health improved a little. His skin looked a normal color again, and he could breathe evenly instead of having to struggle for every breath.

On the fourth day after their arrival the couple participated in a special celebration. The speaker called the day "Christmas" and said, "Two thousand years ago Jesus Christ, the son of God, was born as a human baby on this earth. This Jesus is God's priceless gift to all people."

Prakash and Sumati looked at each other. God's priceless gift! Priceless—that was the name they had given their little son: Amol! Amol meant "priceless" in their language.

Three days later Amol was able to leave the hospital. His parents received some medicine for him, with which he would be able to survive until he was old enough to have surgery. Every time the parents looked at their little Amol they remembered the priceless gift of the Christian God. And they decided they wanted to know more about that God.

This story is based on a true incident.

12: Joseph
Jerusalem, Israel – under Roman rule

Slowly the little caravan started moving again. Still exhausted from the long, steep, dusty ascent up from Jericho, they wandered in a long line at a leisurely pace down the Mount of Olives. Closely behind the leader and his mother, Joseph led the donkey that carried Mary. This way his wife, who was so far advanced in pregnancy, didn't have to walk up that strenuous mountain. It had still been tiring enough for her.

Halfway down the mountain Joseph pointed at a small cone-shaped building with his free hand. "Look, Mary; that's Absalom's tomb."

Mary turned her head in that direction. "That looks very pretty for a tomb! Like an upside-down blossom!"

Soon they reached the bottom of the Kidron Valley, crossed the brook Kidron and climbed up to the city. The difference in height of about one hundred feet was hardly worth mentioning compared with the former strain. But the travelers nevertheless felt the exhaustion and took their time.

The caravan stopped outside the walls near the Pool of Bethesda. Joseph helped Mary off the donkey and gave the animal back to Uzziel, the leader of the caravan. "I can't express how grateful I am to you and your mother for your kind care! This way it was so much easier for Mary."

"Don't even mention it," Uzziel smiled, and his mother added, "We were happy to do it!" Both wished them a safe journey onwards and said goodbye.

Joseph and Mary thanked them again and turned to the city. On their left the enormous wall of the temple precinct towered above them; in front of them the city wall rose. They entered the narrow streets through the Benjamin Gate.

When they had left behind the Roman Fortress of Antonia, that watched over the sanctuary at the northwestern corner of the temple precinct, Joseph asked, "How tired are you, Mary? How much farther are you able to walk today?"

"I had the privilege of riding the whole way today." She smiled up to him. "So I can still walk some more. Why do you ask?"

"I've got a distant relation living in the Lower City where we could stay overnight. But it's still quite a walk. He lives at the southern end of town near the Pool of Siloam."

"I'm sure I'll make it. It'll still be daylight for quite a while so we don't need to hurry, do we?"

"No, we won't have to rush." While they turned to the south and slowly pushed through the crowds of people filling the streets, he again and again looked searchingly into her face to make sure he wouldn't overstrain her.

Abishua and his family welcomed the two travelers gladly. They immediately had their feet washed and their hosts offered them something refreshing to drink. After supper Abishua's wife prepared a bed for the travelers, and they stretched themselves out on it, snuggling tight into the extra blankets their hostess had given them for the cold night.

The next morning Joseph and Mary first walked up the Temple Mount. After washing themselves in the bathhouse that had been built for the cleansing of the pilgrims they slowly ascended the stairs to the eastern Triple Gate. Behind the gate they entered the tunnel, walked through it under the royal columned hall and at the end got to the stairs that led to the Court of the Gentiles.

The noise of construction sounded from many sides as there was still building going on in the temple precinct. The noise of the stonemasons and other craftsmen mixed with the shouting of the money changers, the bleating of the sheep and the lowing of the oxen. The animals were sold to pilgrims to use as offerings.

With difficulty Joseph and Mary wound their way through the crowd and at last passed through the stone gate through which only the Jews could enter. They walked into the Court of the Women where Mary had to stay behind.

"I won't stay long," Joseph assured her. He ascended the steps hewn in a half circle up to the Great Gate. In the Court of the Israelites he placed himself in a spot where Mary could still see him from where she stood. Then he began to pray, "Lord, our great and almighty God! I thank you for your protection on the journey up till here. You kept your protecting hand above us, and I want to praise and extol you for that. Please, protect us also on the onward journey and bring us safely there. I also want to ask you, Lord, to grant me wisdom and strength to care properly for Mary and the child and to protect them. Praise be to your name!"

He remained standing several more minutes in quiet meditation. Then he turned around and walked quickly back to Mary. Together they left the temple precinct through the western Double Gate, descended the wide stairway and wandered through the narrow streets of the city out into the southern direction where Bethlehem was situated.

After some time they saw a village on a hill in front of them, a little to one side. Mary pointed at it with her finger. "That's Beth-Haccherem where I visited my relative half a year ago. After the angel had told me about my son, I spent three months with her. She was also expecting."

Joseph looked at the village and then at Mary. He had caught something in her voice. "Would you like to visit her?" he asked. "It's not a big detour. But you'd have to climb up that hill."

"Oh, I'm sure I'll make it," Mary assured, smiling. "It's not that high."

Less than half an hour later they knocked at the gate to the priest's home. Zechariah opened the door himself and welcomed them gladly. Elizabeth came rushing to the door and greeted Mary, "How wonderful to see you! I so often thought of you. Come in!" She pulled the visitor inside and pointed to a woolen blanket on the floor on which a baby was sleeping. "Look, our little John! By now he's already more than five months old."

"How cute!" Mary looked down at the infant. He woke up, saw the friendly face above him, smiled and waved his arms and legs. And he gurgled happily.

"I'm sure he realized whom you are carrying inside you, like when you visited me before," Elizabeth whispered to Mary, bent down and lifted the child into her arms. Cheerfully the two women played with and entertained the little boy.

Joseph, whom Zechariah had drawn into a conversation, watched Mary surreptitiously. Somehow she seemed weary and fatigued despite her cheerfulness.

After having some refreshments, Joseph reminded her that they must leave. He noticed the shadow spreading across Mary's face. But immediately she got up.

"Oh, you can't go so soon!" Elizabeth protested. "You've just arrived! Bethlehem isn't that far; it won't take you long."

"I want to find a secure lodging before nightfall," Joseph explained.

"Why don't you stay overnight?" Zechariah asked. "If you leave in the morning you've got enough time to look for something."

Joseph looked at Mary to find out what she thought about that suggestion. But she was staring at the floor. Maybe she didn't want to influence his decision.

He thought about it briefly, then agreed to stay. Mary lifted her head, and when he saw her eyes lighting up he knew that he had decided the way she wanted it. "But only one night," he added. "I want to be settled securely before Mary's hour is at hand."

"Are you really that far along?" Elizabeth looked at her young relative, surprised.

"Probably only two more weeks," Mary confirmed.

"Oh my, is it that long ago that you stayed with me? Since John was born time seems to just fly. I didn't realize how many months have passed since then...although I should've been able to know because of John's age," she added, laughing.

In the course of the next morning Joseph and Mary started for Bethlehem. "The land around here must be very fertile." Mary pointed to the freshly ploughed grain fields through which they were wandering. On some of them farmers were walking, sowing seeds with their hands.

"Yes, the soil is very good," Joseph confirmed. "I also own a little piece. It probably lies fallow unless one of my relatives that still live here is caring for it."

As Bethlehem was situated on a hill, the path started to go up again. Soon Joseph noticed that Mary's steps became slower. Exhaustion was written on her face.

The sun had already passed its highest point when they reached the town. Joseph led Mary into a small lane and stopped in front of one of the whitewashed houses. "This is where Gemariah lives. He's a mason like me, and we share the same grandparents. Gemariah's mother was my father's sister. As my relative he'll surely make some room for us!" Joseph knocked at the gate.

A confusion of voices could be heard but nobody opened. "It seems we're not the first relatives that came for the census," Joseph remarked and knocked a little more loudly. When even that didn't help he used his fist against the wooden door. A little later the gate swung open, and a young man of Joseph's age stood in the doorway. "Joseph! It's you! Welcome!" he shouted when he recognized his cousin.

Then he looked at Mary. His broad smile faded, and a shadow ran across his face. Joseph saw it, and he suspected the meaning. His throat constricted, and he tried hard to clear it. "Thank you, Gemariah, for your kind welcome. God bless you!" Pointing to Mary he added, "This is Mary, my wife. We came because of the census."

"That's what I thought." Gemariah frowned. "My house is already full with relatives who have come for just that reason. Under normal circumstances I would gladly offer you a place even if it was my own bed. But now..." His eyes traveled across Mary's big abdomen. Then he looked at Joseph, his eyes asking for understanding. "You know the law. Because of the birth the whole house with everybody in it would become unclean. I'd drive out all my guests. You surely understand..." His voice trailed away.

By now Basemath had stepped beside her husband and had heard his last words. She looked at Mary, sighed, and then turned to Joseph. "The whole village is filled to overflowing with people who came because of the census. Therefore I'm afraid nobody will be able to take you in. But if you follow this lane here..." She pointed towards the left with her hand. "...then you'll find a cave directly behind the village where we keep our animals overnight. The cave is warm and dry and quite safe. There you could stay. I'll send my servant girl with blankets and food so that you'll have something to eat and can have a soft bed. And if you need more just let me know. I'm very sorry we can't offer you more but under the circumstances..." She lifted her hands and smiled apologetically. "May God bless and keep you!"

"Thank you, both." Joseph bowed down and turned to Mary. "Come! I know which cave Basemath is talking about. Let's go there so that you can at last lie down and get some rest."

13: Calum
Isle of Lewis, Scotland – ca. 1965

With a mighty roar, the waves of the Atlantic Ocean broke against the steep, rocky walls on either side of the small inlet of Cliobh[12], splashing several yards into the air. No obstacle hindered the sea from smashing against the northwest coast of Leodhas[13], the biggest island in the Scottish Outer Hebrides. The water crashed onto the small sandy beach and climbed higher and higher up towards the tiny village. The storm was caught between the rock walls and roared around the few houses of Cliobh.

Five-year-old Calum stood at the window and gazed at the furious, raging sea. "Mummy, can the water come up to our house?" His voice betrayed fear.

"I hope not. I've never experienced such a terrible storm, not since I moved here six years ago when I married your father." The mother threw an uneasy glance out of the window.

"Mummy, can the storm crush our house?"

"Surely not! It's built out of big, sturdy blocks of stone. They can weather any storm."

"And the roof? Can it be blown away? Then we'll get all wet!"

"No, I don't think so. The heather's covered with a strong net, and that is secured with heavy stones."

For a moment Calum seemed reassured. Then he turned around and asked in a mournful voice, "Mummy, is Daddy out there in that awful storm?"

The mother didn't answer immediately. She stepped towards the window, stood beside Calum, stared a while at the thundering water, and sighed. Then she took her son by the hand, sat down on a chair and pulled the boy onto her lap. "Yes, Calum," she said, and her voice trembled.

---

[12] English name: Cliff
[13] English name: Lewis

"Daddy's out there. Last night he went out with Uncle Norman to catch some fish. He hasn't returned yet, though it's already noontime."

"Why did he have to go along this time? He isn't a fisherman like Uncle Norman."

"No, he isn't. But you know that he joins his brother sometimes so that we can have some fish to eat without having to buy it."

"But why today when there is such a storm! That's dangerous! What if their boat turns over?"

"When Daddy left there was no sign of a storm. The sea was pretty calm."

"But it's not calm now!" Calum leaned against his mother. "Oh, if something happens to Daddy! Oh Mummy, I'm so scared!"

"Me too," the mother admitted in a low voice. "We can only hope that Daddy and Uncle Norman found shelter on one of the islets off West Loch Roag. Come, let's ask God to protect our Daddy."

Calum folded his little hands, and the mother put her hands around his. Then she asked God for protection for the two men.

The storm raged on until night descended. It only calmed down about the time when the mother dressed herself and her son in their warm winter coats to go to the Christmas service that was to start at 11 p.m. in the church in Miabhig[14]. Mairi (MEH-ree), Calum's two-year-old sister, stayed at home with their grandmother. The distance was too much for her short legs. And the father who would have carried her still hadn't returned.

The mother held a lantern in her right hand while her left closed around Calum's small hand. Outside the house the neighbors joined them. Silently the small group marched through the night to the next village that guarded the entrance to their peninsula.

---

[14] English name: Miavaig

Most of the way Loch Sgailler (SGEL-lah) lay on their right, a narrow but long lake. Calum was relieved that his mother was walking between him and the black, quietly gurgling water. It looked so spooky in the darkness of the night. He preferred the rock wall on his left, although it towered dark and menacing at his side.

Thick clouds sailed across the night sky and allowed only brief glimpses of a few stars. The moon was nowhere to be seen. Even before they reached the doctor's house, the first building of Miabhig, it started to drizzle.

At the doctor's house they met the women and children of Uigean[15] coming out of the side road with their lanterns. Aunt Ishbal, Uncle Norman's wife, and her two sons Duncan and Donald quickly joined Calum and his mother. The aunt whispered hurriedly, "About an hour ago when the storm died down all the men of Uigean went out with their boats. Oh, Hannah! I hope they'll find them!"

"Yes, I hope so, too!" Calum's mother answered quietly and walked on with her sister-in-law. Soon they reached the church. Before entering they cast a long look across the wide dark water to the point where the bay turned left in a sweeping bend to the open sea. Not the tiniest dot of light was visible, only black water and deep darkness. The women looked at each other worriedly.

On his seat in the church pew, Calum pressed himself against his mother. When she put her arm around him he felt her trembling. He could hardly suppress a sob. In less than an hour Christmas Day would begin. Would they have to live through it without their father? Maybe forever?

Neither his mother nor his aunt or cousins joined in the singing of the Psalms. All five of them sat silent and motionless in the pew. Only when the minister prayed for God's protection and rescue for the men out at sea, they whispered an amen.

Just before the end of the service the church door was thrown open. A man in drenched clothes looked hurriedly around, then hastened to the village doctor who stood up

---

[15] English name: Uigen

quickly. On his way out he spotted Calum's mother and aunt in the back pew and signaled to them before he rushed out with the doctor.

Clinging to his mother's hand, Calum ran after the light of the two men as fast as his short legs allowed. Aunt Ishbal, Duncan, and Donald followed close behind.

The two men disappeared into the doctor's house. Breathlessly the women and children reached the front door after them. The men of Uigean sat in the kitchen warming themselves with hot tea after their night's search. Mr. MacLeod jumped up and stepped towards the five newcomers. "No need to worry," he soothed. "We found them. Everything's alright. The doctor's checking on them."

"Where...where did you find them?" Aunt Ishbal asked in a husky voice.

"Way out on An t-Seana Bheinn[16]. They were still on the outer sea when the storm surprised them. And then they were driven directly into the little sandy inlet of An t-Seana Bheinn. That was the best thing that could have happened to them. They don't have injuries, but severe hypothermia. They were so stiff by the time we got there that we had to carry them into the boat. But that will mend. Thank God!"

"Yes, thanks to God!" Calum felt his mother's hand tighten around his when she said this. "God heard our prayers. But I shall never forget this Christmas!"

"Nor will I," whispered Calum and looked up at his mother.

---

[16] English name: Old Hill

14: Caitlin
Isle of Lewis, Scotland – ca. 2000

Caitlin crouched down on the beach and let the damp, whitish-yellow sand glide through her fingers absent-mindedly. In a thoughtful mood she looked out over the sea. During summer the water shimmered in a strong turquoise-blue color near the beach, changing more and more into deep blue outside the cove of Cliobh[17]. That is, if the sun shone from a blue sky. If not, especially if there was a storm raging, the waves hurried in–as they were doing now–in dismal gray, broke thundering on the steep rock walls left and right of the cove, threw themselves roaring and foaming onto the beach. Shivering, Caitlin remembered what her grandmother had told her: Many years ago her grandfather had been surprised out on the sea by such a storm when he and his brother had gone out fishing the day before Christmas.

This cove was full of dangers in summer and in winter. That's why swimming was prohibited at all times. Today, only two days after winter solstice, it was too cold anyway. It seldom snowed or froze on Leodhas[18], the largest and northernmost island of the Hebrides of Scotland, because the Gulf Stream warmed the water. But now, in December, strong winds and dull, damp weather kept everybody indoors who did not need to go out.

Caitlin also did not stay long at the water. The rising tide drove the waves farther and farther onto the beach and would soon reach her feet. She jumped up, climbed the slope and ran to her parent's house.

She found her mother and Catherine, her older sister, in the kitchen preparing the Christmas dinner. As Caitlin would only be in the way, she withdrew to her seanmhair[19]

---

[17] English name: Cliff
[18] English name: Lewis
[19] Gaelic for grandmother, pronounced SHEHN-vair

and crouched down in front of the fireplace. How cozy and warm the peat fire glowed and shone. Caitlin breathed deeply and inhaled the sweet smell. Then she turned around to her grandmother.

"Seanag[20], tell me about earlier times: How you celebrated Christmas. Long ago when you were a little girl. Did you also drive to Miabhig[21] to the village hall in the evening and celebrate there with all the other people?"

"Oh no, child, when I was your age everything was different. And I didn't grow up here in Cliobh but on Bearnaraigh[22]; you know, the island in Loch Roag between here and Charlabhaig[23]."

"Oh, please, Seanag, tell me about it, how it was so different."

"Well, you know, Caitlin, there's nothing nice to tell about the time I was your age. But then something very special happened, and that changed our whole family. Yes, it influenced and totally changed even the life of the entire island."

"Something special? O Seanag, please, please, tell me about it!"

"Well, Caitlin, as I said before, life was not pleasant at all when I was as young as you are now. We were very, very poor. My father was a fisherman. When he got some money from selling fish he often went to the pub and spent all that money on alcohol. And when he came home drunk he raged and beat us, on Christmas even more than on other days. No, it wasn't pleasant at all!"

The grandmother shivered with the memory, sighed, and stared silently out of the window for quite a while.

"Go on, Seanag," Caitlin begged. "What happened then?"

"Yes, what happened then," the grandmother repeated and stroked her forehead with her hand as if she had to

---

[20] Gaelic for Grandma, pronounced SHEHN-egg
[21] English name: Miavaig
[22] English name: Bernera
[23] English name: Carloway

push away the ugly memory. "Then something happened that was so unusual, so great that I don't know how to describe it." She stopped again.

"Go on, Seanag!" Caitlin pressed. She pulled her legs up, put her arms around them and rested her chin on her knees. Expectantly she looked up at her grandmother.

The old woman smiled. "Oh Caitlin, I'll never forget that day. A preacher from the mainland had already preached for some time in Barabhas[24] and Arnol at the northern coast of Leodhas, and strange rumors had reached us. Then he got to Calanais[25], and there people also told wonderful things. Calanais, you know, where those old stone circles are, isn't very far from Bearnaraigh. And one day he crossed to Bearanraigh in a boat..."

"Why didn't he drive across the bridge?" Caitlin interrupted.

"At that time the bridge wasn't built yet; it all happened more than fifty years ago. It must've been around 1950; I was thirteen or so." The grandmother stopped and thought about it.

"Doesn't matter how old you were! Just go on, please!"

"Well, yes, this preacher came to our village as well. My mother took us children along to the communion service while my father again went to the pub. It felt very strange in the church—somehow depressing. In the middle of the sermon the preacher stopped, looked at a boy who was maybe three or four years older than me and asked him to pray.

"The boy got up and prayed something about an open door into heaven that he was seeing with his inner eyes, and something about a lamb with a set of keys.

"For a short moment everything was deadly quiet. Then the boy lifted his head and asked God to show his power."

Caitlin hardly dared to breathe. "And then?" she whispered.

---

[24] English name: Barvas
[25] English name: Callanish

"Then..." The grandmother inhaled deeply. "Then the...the Spirit of God came into our midst. We couldn't see him but we all sensed him. The people began to weep and confessed their sin because they had not obeyed God but lived to fulfill their own desires and ideas. And this knowledge not only got to us in the church. No, the whole village and beyond got into its grip at the same time. Later when we went home we saw our father sitting on the side of the road. God's presence had overpowered him so that he hadn't even been able to get to church. For several days people hardly went to work because they were so intent on seeking God's grace and forgiveness.

"Yes, Caitlin, that's how it happened. Our whole lives, not only on Bearnaraigh but in many parts of Leadhas, were totally changed by this revival. Even today you can sense and see the results. The churches are full, and on Sundays no plane is allowed to land in Steornabhagh[26] and no ferry arrives in port[27]. The day of the Lord is kept quiet and with dignity.

"And...and what about your father? Had he...could he...?"

"Even he was changed completely. He became a loving and good father who faithfully cared for his family. Christmas had lost its horror. Instead we celebrated it in silent devotion and quiet peace. At midnight we all gathered in church and praised God who came down to earth so that we could have forgiveness and new life."

---

[26] English name: Stornoway
[27] This changed only in 2013

15: Lydia
Cape Town, South Africa – 1982

"Today's Christmas Eve," seven-year-old Lydia informed her younger siblings.

"Oh, yeah!" Marcus shouted excitedly. Only a few weeks ago he had celebrated his fourth birthday. "I'll get even more presents!" And he turned his back on Lydia to concentrate on the large toy truck he had received for his birthday. After loading it with Lego blocks he drove it noisily to his Lego construction site.

Lydia turned to Sarah and Maren (MAH-rehn), the 18-month-old twins. "Today's Christmas Eve," she repeated. But the little girls didn't care. Last Christmas they had still been babies and couldn't remember anything about it.

"We'll get lots of presents," Lydia tried to explain. "And there'll be a tree with lots of lights! And chocolate dominoes and chocolate hearts! And...and..." She faltered and then continued slowly in a low voice, "And Oma[28] always brought a huge tin full of cookies that she'd baked for us. And outside it was cold...not as...as hot as here!"

Abruptly Lydia turned around and ran into the kitchen. "Mami[29], I don't feel like Christmas at all," she complained. "At home it was so much nicer; it was really cold and it even snowed a little. But here it's strange. Christmas shouldn't be this hot!"

The mother gently stroked Lydia's hair. "It's because we're on the other side of the globe. Germany is north of the equator, so it's winter there now. But here in Cape Town in South Africa we're on the southern side, so it's summer now."

"Why did we have to come here? We could've stayed in Germany, couldn't we?"

---

[28] German for Grandma, pronounced OH-mah
[29] German for Mommy, pronounced MAH-mee

"Oh Lydia, you know exactly why we're here, don't you?" her mother rebuked her. "We want to tell these people about Jesus. So many don't know him yet."

Lydia mumbled something to herself and then became silent. After a while she asked, "So what are we going to do today?"

"Papi's[30] going to go to the beach with you soon so you can go swimming. And for the afternoon we're planning something special."

The girl spun around and stomped out of the kitchen. "Swimming," she hissed. "Go to the beach! On Christmas Eve!!"

An hour later she was sitting on the beach frowning while she watched her younger siblings enjoying the water with their father. They didn't seem to care about celebrating Christmas in such a totally different way than back home in Germany. Their happy squeals could be heard along the whole beach. Everywhere there were people swimming in the water or lying in the sun. Some started unpacking their picnic lunches.

Lydia squinted at the sun burning down on her. *Christmas in summer! It just isn't right. How can I look forward to the evening[31]?* Her mother's promise of a special afternoon didn't cheer her up. That couldn't be anything nice, could it?

When they returned home a waft of Christmassy fragrance greeted them, smelling of gingerbread and cinnamon. With shouts of joy Marcus ran to the kitchen, followed by the twins. Only Lydia held back. Everything in her rebelled against such a "wrong Christmas", as she called it to herself.

After lunch the mother asked her oldest, "Come, Lydia, you're my big girl. Will you help me?"

The girl only nodded. Silently she handed her mother the many parcels that were wrapped in pretty Christmas paper. The mother carefully packed them into a big bas-

---

[30] German for Daddy, pronounced PAH-pee
[31] In Germany Christmas Eve is the main celebration; the gifts are opened then.

ket. On the handle she tied a bright red ribbon. "That's it. Now we've only got to change, and then we're ready."

Lydia was old enough to dress herself in her white festive dress while the mother helped Marcus and the twins into their summer finery. The father carried the heavy basket to the car, and the kids climbed into the back seats.

"Papi, where're we going?" Marcus asked when the father pulled out onto the highway.

"To Mitchell's Plain," the father replied.

"Yeah!" Marcus shouted. "I've always wanted to go there."

Lydia didn't utter a word. She hadn't been there either. But their father had told them about it. Mitchell's Plain–that was the beautiful new part of the city the government had built for the "Coloured people", so they could move out of their awful old huts infested with poisonous snakes and terrible diseases. "Coloured", the father had explained, is what the people in South Africa are called who have parents from different races, like a white father and a black mother or the other way around. These "Coloured people" then married other "Coloured people", and soon there were quite a lot of them. The black people didn't like them because they weren't fully black, and the whites despised them because they weren't fully white. But Lydia's parents felt God's call to go to these people and tell them about God's wonderful love.

After they had entered the area, the girl looked curiously out of the window. There, that must be the beautiful shopping center her father had told her about. Many people, with skin darker than Lydia's, rushed in and out of the big doors. Those that came out were laden with parcels and bags.

They passed the shopping center and turned into a side street. On both sides of the road there were long rows of two-story houses. They stopped in front of a corner house and climbed out of the car. The father led the way, carrying the heavy basket. At the front door he knocked.

A few seconds later Lydia heard steps, the door was opened a crack, then flung open. A woman in a bright red dress was smiling broadly at them.

"Merry Christmas, Mrs. Manasa[32]!" the father greeted the woman.

"Merry Christmas!" the woman answered. "Please, come in."

The German missionary family stepped into the sitting room. Mr. Manasa was sitting there, surrounded by his nine children. They greeted their visitors loudly and with happy laughter. Two of the older girls took the twins onto their laps, and Marcus immediately started talking to a boy his own age.

Lydia was trying to hide behind her mother when a girl her age took her hand. "Come, sit with me. My name's Lucy. What's yours?"

"My name is...is Lydia."

The two girls sat down on the carpet. Lydia's father started singing a Christmas carol, and all the others joined in–all except Lydia.

They sang several songs, loudly and lively, and clapped their hands to the rhythms. Later Lydia's father opened his Bible and read the Christmas story of how God's son was born in poverty and how the angels praised God. Lydia's father prayed, then they sang again–all except Lydia.

While the others were singing, Lydia sat in their midst. Slowly the anger and disappointment she had felt since the morning began to fade away. And when later on, her mother distributed the gifts out of her basket and Lydia saw and heard the happiness of the many children, she took a deep breath. Suddenly she understood that the joy of Christmas didn't depend on a tree and snow and Grandma's cookies, but on the child in the manger. This child was God's magnificent gift to people all over the world. And this gift could be enjoyed in any place!

---

[32] pronounced mah-NAH-sah

16: Harimaya
Khani, Nepal – ca. 1990

Harimaya (hah-ree-MY-ah) and Ranjeeta (rahn-JEE-tah), her best friend, were chatting happily as they stood looking up the mountain slope expectantly. A moment later, Bhim Bahadur (BIM bah-hah-DURE) and the other older village boys appeared out of the forest, leading the sheep before them. During the summer the sheep grazed at a height of around fifteen thousand feet. But now in December they were brought down to Khani. Most of this Nepalese village was built at a height of forty-three hundred feet, but many of the houses stood further up the mountain. Their walls still shone in fresh and beautiful colors: red or yellow or green on the bottom, with white above. Only two months ago, they had been painted afresh to celebrate the Hindu festival of Dashain (dah-SHINE).

"Will it snow soon?" Harimaya squinted up to Kumbhakarna (koom-bah-KAR-nah), towering at twenty-five thousand feet above her. The top was covered in clouds, and below them the snow glistened in a white radiance.

"I don't know," Ranjeeta shrugged her shoulders. "Look, there's Bhim Bahadur, ahead of everybody else. As usual!" Ranjeeta would have loved to discover Harimaya's oldest brother's opinion of her. Although her secret wishes were likely to remain unfulfilled: Only very rarely did young men select a bride from their own village.

"Tonight we're going to the Christian youth group that Ram Chandra (RAHM CHAHN-drah) started when he came back from college. Will you come along?"

Ranjeeta shook her head. "Are you going?"

"Yes." Harimaya nodded. "Bhim Bahadur is taking me. You're very welcome to join us!" Wouldn't that be tempting enough for her friend?

"What are you going to do there?"

"Oh, it's lovely there. We go twice a week; we sing together, listen to something out of the Christian holy book–they call it Bible–and then they pray to their God. Why don't you come along and see for yourself?"

"Well, no...it's too dangerous."

"Dangerous? Why?"

"It's forbidden," Ranjeeta explained. "My father says that in other villages people were thrown in prison because they became Christians. That can happen here as well! The only reason why they haven't done anything yet is because Ram Chandra is the son of the village chief."

"I'll go anyway. I like it there, and I want to hear more about the Christian God. But now I need to go and help my mother. It's already four o'clock; soon my sisters will be home from school. They don't usually need more than an hour to come up from down there."

She said goodbye and hurried home. A few minutes later Kamala (kah-MAH-lah) and Gaumaya (gah-oo-MY-ah), her two youngest sisters, came running through the door.

"Look what we've got!" they exclaimed, holding an orange each in their hands.

"Did you pick those?" their mother frowned.

"No, no, they were lying on the ground," Gaumaya hurriedly explained. "Last night there was a hailstorm down in that village, and the hail knocked down lots of oranges. So we picked some up because we can't grow any up here."

Their mother looked at the fruit. "Put them over there. They aren't ripe yet. And then come to eat. The kholi is ready." She set the millet gruel on the table.

After this snack Harimaya helped her mother prepare the hot evening meal. While she ground chili and ginger she thought about Ranjeeta's words of warning. Was it really so dangerous to attend those Christian youth gatherings? Two of the primary school teachers even went there. And she liked it. This mighty God, Ram Chandra had explained, was the only true God. He had created everything: the high majestic mountains, the countless rhododendrons that covered large areas of the mountain slopes with their beautiful bright red blossoms in spring, the apple trees and the delicious strawberries in the forest, the wheat, the millet, the corn, the barley and the potatoes that grew on the fields around Khani, the cows, the buffaloes, sheep and goats which gave them milk for nourishment, wool for clothing and leather for shoes, and, of course, the people, her parents, siblings, the whole tribe of the Limbu and so many others about whom Harimaya had learned at school. All of this, God had created! And even better than that: God loved all these people, cared for them and wanted to help them. *No, Harimaya thought, I won't stay away. I need to learn more about this God – a God who loves me and whom I need not fear!*

After the evening meal, she and Bhim Bahadur went to the village chief's big house. The wooden shutters were already closed to keep the cold night air out. In December, the temperatures could drop down to the freezing point. Harimaya pulled her densely woven woolen cardigan more tightly around herself. But among the eighteen young people who had gathered, she soon stopped shivering.

"Today I need to tell you a special story," Ram Chandra began, after they had been singing loudly and cheerfully for a while. And then he told the story about how God decided to come down to earth and become a man so that the people could understand his message. So that he would know how humans live and feel, he was born as a little baby named Jesus into a poor family. Ram Chandra read the story from Luke's gospel and also added the story about the wise men from the Gospel of Matthew. Then he explained what all this meant for the people of Khani.

Oh no! They even wanted to kill God's own son as a baby, Harimaya thought. *How terrible! Should we be surprised, then, if they put his followers into prison? But God protected his son, and he'll help us, too. He's so different and so much better than anything I've known so far!* She went on listening attentively.

"Every year in December, Christians around the world remember this holy night and celebrate," Ram Chandra said in closing. "That's why I wanted to tell you about it today. Now we can join in the celebration!"

17: Jean-Luc
Haiti – ca. 1980

"Imagine, we're going away from here!" Eight-year-old Jean-Luc ran to meet Pierre, his neighbor boy, who was a little older than him.

"Ah!" Pierre frowned. "And where are you planning to go?"

"To the big village down on the road to Port-au-Prince."

"And what do you intend to do there?"

"We'll move in with my uncle Placide, into his house." Jean-Luc's brown eyes sparkled in his dark face.

"Oh?" Pierre pushed his hands into the pockets of his shorts. "And why are you doing that?"

"He's richer than we are. Recently he built an additional room where my aunt can build her fire so that she no longer needs to cook outside like my mother has to."

"That's really something. But are you sure your uncle'll want to have you?"

"My aunt's my mother's older sister. So he has to care for us."

Pierre made a face. "Well, good luck! We wouldn't be happy if suddenly my mother's relatives would appear at our door to live with us."

"They're richer than we are if they have an extra room in which to cook." Jean-Luc stuck out his lower lip. "We've only two rooms for eating and sleeping."

"Most of the people around here have that. Hardly anybody can afford more."

"But my uncle can," Jean-Luc shouted and stomped his naked foot on the ground.

"It's okay. I believe you," Pierre tried to calm him and grinned. Then he looked intently at Jean-Luc and put his hand on his shoulder. "Remember, Jean-Luc! Don't walk under the Sablié tree." He turned around and hurried off.

Jean-Luc ran his hand through his black curls and sighed while he watched Pierre run away. Then he also turned around and trotted home. In his thoughts he was still with Pierre. "Don't walk under the Sablié tree," his friend had reminded him. That meant something like "Don't forget me! Don't forget where you come from!" To walk or stand under a Sablié (sah-blee-AY) tree meant to forget the past. Jean-Luc believed that just as much as most people in Haiti.

No, I don't want to forget Pierre, Jean-Luc determined. *He's my friend. I'll miss him. But...will my uncle really take us in?*

At home everything was ready for leaving. Marie-Claude, Jean-Luc's five-year-old sister, carried their little brother on her back. The father walked in front; after him came the mother with the children. They made their way down the steep mountain with difficulty. Large, bright red poinsettias painted colorful spots on the barren slope.

Farther down Jean-Luc discovered pineapple plants, and a little later they walked through a banana grove. The whole family enjoyed the little shade in the hot Caribbean sun. Under the cool shade of a walnut tree they rested a bit before they walked on.

Dusk had begun when they neared their destination. The merchants along the road were lighting the little candles in the artistically decorated paper lanterns that had not yet been sold. Today on the Holy Eve was their last chance to earn some money with them.

It's true, Jean-Luc thought when they saw their uncle's hut appear. *He really has built an extra room for cooking...Oh, there's Esther!*

His cousin looked out of the door to the main building. She held a broom made from banana leaves in her hand as she had just finished sweeping the hut clean for the Christmas celebration. When she saw the Lorquet (lor-KEH) family approaching, she turned around and disappeared into the hut. A moment later the uncle was standing in the door.

Full of suspense Jean-Luc followed the talk of the two men. The uncle frowned and looked around at each of the family members. He didn't seem too happy about the unexpected visitors. Then he murmured something about "wait" and retreated into the house. Jean-Luc heard some voices talk together inside the house but could hardly understand anything. Only a few broken pieces of words made their way outside. Once he recognized the name "Jesus", then they seemed to talk about "God". What did that have to do with their arrival?

At last the uncle opened the door again, smiling now, and with a move of his hand invited them in. Jean-Luc entered the room with his family. The room did not look much different than at home. Besides the simple wooden table and a few chairs made from wood there were no other pieces of furniture. Was the uncle really that much richer? But he had that additional room!

At midnight both families went to church. Jean-Luc joined his cousin Joseph. He saw with astonishment that they didn't go to the Catholic church but to another unknown building. It was decorated with colorful paper just as he was used to. But they sang totally different songs. And how they sang! Never had Jean-Luc heard such joyful, lively singing.

And the sermon! It sounded so different than anything he had heard until now. Of course he knew that at Christmas they celebrated the birth of baby Jesus. But nobody had ever told him so clearly about the reason why Jesus was born into our world. And he also hadn't known that this child Jesus welcomed everybody who came to him. He wasn't sure what that meant.

After the service they shared a meal in the uncle's house. Besides rice and black beans, Jean-Luc spotted chicklies, a very hot and spicy sauce, on the table. When his aunt added cabrite (kah-BREET)–fried mutton–to it, Jean-Luc stared openmouthed. Now he no longer doubted the wealth of his uncle.

When his uncle smilingly invited the whole family to eat, Jean-Luc suddenly understood what the pastor had meant.

Just as his uncle had opened his door to them and invited them in, so Jesus had, by coming down to earth, opened the door to Heaven and invited everybody in. Jean-Luc decided that he had to tell Pierre about that. At the next opportunity he wanted to go see his friend and tell him the good news.

18: Tatyana
Upper Volga River, Russia – ca. 1993

Tatyana stood at the window and tried to peek through the ice-covered panes into the gray light of noon. It was around the winter solstice, and as this little village on the upper Volga river somewhere between Yaroslavl and Kostroma lay very far north, the day allowed less than four hours of light to man and nature. And even this little bit of light stayed dim and dull.

In front of the window the Volga flowed past lazily. Although the way to the mouth of the river where it flowed into the Caspian Sea was still very far–more than twelve hundred miles–it already had grown into a mighty river. The gloomy song of the Volga bargemen, which in summer so often was heard across the water, had become silent. Only the white, still world of winter stretched across the banks and kept the wide north Russian landscape tightly in its grip.

How beautiful the summer had been in the large garden–full of flowers that gladdened heart and eyes, but also full of fruit and vegetables that filled the stomach. And part of this blessing, what they had not been able to eat yet, was stored well in the cellar of the blue-painted wooden house to carry the family through the winter. The empty garden now slumbered under the snow awaiting a new spring.

Behind Tatyana, in the dimly lit room, her grandmother sat. She held her calloused hands folded in her lap and watched her six-year-old granddaughter. The child had been standing at the window for quite a while, breathing against the pane again and again and struggling to keep the little peephole open.

"Babushka[33]?" Tatyana looked up at the slim, graceful, frozen birches that flanked the fence like a row of geese. "Why do trees have no leaves in winter?"

"Because in fall they become old and withered and yellow and fall off. Leaves live only for one summer. The following year their children grow."

"But why do they live only such a short time?" Tatyana wrinkled her forehead.

"I don't know, Sweetie."

For a while it was quiet in the room. Then Tatyana complained, "Babushka, I'm bored. Will you tell me a story?"

"Well, yes, Girlie, come to me!"

Tatyana left the window, tripped over to the bench by the stove and pushed herself up onto her grandmother's lap. She slung one arm around the furrowed neck of the old woman and leaned her head against the beloved shoulder.

The grandmother put her arms around her granddaughter and told her about the holy child that was born almost two thousand years ago on a cold winter's night among the animals in the stable. "And soon we all will go to church to celebrate his birth," she concluded.

Dressed warmly in coats and head scarves, the father wearing his fur hat, the whole family trudged along the road to church in the moonlight. The parents went first. Mommy carried Alexei, Tatyana's almost two-year-old little brother, in her arms. Tatyana followed with her grandmother, her little hand put into Babushka's right one. Innumerable stars were shining from the sky. Was the star of Bethlehem among them?

The Orthodox village church had only been reopened last spring after being closed for seventy years and services being forbidden. But now even a priest had returned. The villagers had tried to renovate the dilapidated building as best as possible, and now at last they again had regular services in the village.

---

[33] Russian for grandmother

The onion domes stood dark and sharply cut against the moonlight and threw mighty shadows onto the snowy street. In front of the entrance portal the parents and the grandmother stamped their feet to get the snow off, and the girl followed their example, holding tightly to her grandmother's hand so that she would not lose her footing on the slippery ground.

The flitting light of the many burning candles welcomed the newcomers when they entered the sanctuary. Several neighbors were already standing there; others were still arriving. The festive liturgy, which was sung like all Orthodox liturgy, sounded bright and clear, like heavenly bells through the church.

"I can't stand that long," the grandmother whispered to Tatyana. "Would you like to come along?"

The girl nodded. Together they tiptoed as quietly as possible to the back wall along which ran a bench for those who could not remain standing all the many hours a service normally lasted. The grandmother sat down, heaving a sigh of relief. Tatyana sat down beside her cuddling close.

For a while the child looked at the colorful wall paintings, blinked into the candlelight and listened to the beautiful singing. But soon her eyelids became heavy, and she fell asleep. She only woke up when her mother stroked her arm. "Come," she whispered. "We need to go home. Alyosha[34] is getting too restless."

During the service the weather had changed. Dense clouds hid the moon and the stars, and impenetrable darkness waited behind the light that fell through the bulleye panes of the church windows and painted interesting patterns onto the white ground.

The father lit the lantern he always took along in winter. They had hardly left the light that fell from the church windows when it started snowing heavily. The snowflakes glittered silvery white around the lantern.

Tatyana clung to her grandmother's hand. She could hardly see the outlines of her parents in front of her. She

---

[34] Nickname for Alexei

fervently hoped they would not lose them out of sight altogether. How should they find their way without the lantern? Would they then get lost, maybe even walk into the Volga by accident? Onto the ice that had formed at the edges? And which would then break and let them fall into the icy water? Tatyana's heart was beating wildly.

Just a short time ago her grandmother had told her a story, hadn't she, about a boy who had been so foolhardy as to go onto thin ice? He had broken through, had been swept under the ice by the current and drowned. Despite the cold Tatyana felt hot just thinking about it.

The snowfall became more and more dense. A strong wind started to blow. Tatyana had difficulty bracing herself against it. And then suddenly it went totally dark. The storm had blown out the light of the lantern.

Tatyana and her grandmother almost fell because they bumped so strongly into the parents that had stopped abruptly. The father tried hard to relight the lantern. But the storm, growing stronger and stronger, foiled all attempts. When the mother started stomping her feet because she felt colder and colder the father at last gave up. Tatyana didn't know whether she trembled more from cold or more from fear.

"Come, we can't lose each other. Let's link arms," the father admonished. "Tatyana, hang tightly onto my right arm; I still need to carry the lantern. Babushka should hold you from the other side." He himself put his left arm around the shoulders of his wife who carried Alexei.

Hurriedly Tatyana searched for her father's arm and clutched it tightly, while her grandmother closed her hand around her granddaughter's other hand. Step by step they fought their way onwards, hoping not to lose direction.

Through the storm Tatyana heard her grandmother talking to herself. "What did you say, Babushka?" she asked with chattering teeth.

"Nothing, Child. I am only praying to God that he'll soon let us find our way safely home."

Although it didn't take a lot of time it seemed to Tatyana as if they had been walking for hours. Suddenly the grandmother bumped into something hard and shouted, "Stop! Isn't this our fence?"

And it was true! "Thanks to God!" the mother murmured when the father opened the front door and lit a candle inside the house. Shortly after that the oil lamp was lit and spread its soft light.

While the mother cared for Alexei and put him to bed, the grandmother filled the samovar with water, put charcoal into the little oven in the lower part of the samovar and kindled it. The pot with the tea concentrate she put onto the konforka, the little crown on the top beside the chimney of the samovar.

After a while the samovar started to hum and to hiss and to steam. The mother, who had by now joined them, poured some of the strong tea brew into cups and filled them up with boiling water. Oh, how much they enjoyed the hot tea after the cold and the fright! How nicely did the warmth flow through their bodies!

Shuddering, Tatyana thought back to the walk through the darkness. Then she heaved a sigh of relief. "Thank you, dear God," she whispered. "Thank you for hearing and answering Babushka's prayer!"

19: Khaya
Bulawayo, Zimbabwe – ca. 2000

Terror filling her eyes, Khaya stared at the woman that stood in front of her. She knew her, as she lived only a few houses down the road. The houses along the road were poor houses where a whole family of the Ndebele tribe, often even several of them, squeezed into one single room. The air under those corrugated metal roofs was humid in summer and very stuffy. Each of these tiny houses resembled the many others in this part of Bulawayo, the biggest town in Matabeleland, the southern part of Zimbabwe.

What was it that the neighbor had said? Khaya tried hard to grasp the words—and at the same time push them away. It couldn't, it mustn't be true! "Your mother will also die," the woman had said. Hadn't she? It had sounded like a normal statement like, "I need to go shopping," or something like that.

No, no, it simply couldn't be true! Wasn't it enough that her father had died last winter? And before that her uncles and aunts? Her mother was the last of her family that was still alive. But she was sick, too. What should Khaya, her sister Dalitso and Jabulani, their little baby brother, do if their mother left them as well?

"Your mother has AIDS," the neighbor woman had said. "Like your father. And all the others. Your mother will die just like all of them."

Khaya's heart beat painfully. No, this just couldn't happen! Not her mother, her beloved mother! Full of fear she rushed home. But her mother was lying there just the way she had left her in the morning.

Two days later Khaya had to leave home again to trade one of their possessions for something to eat. Soon they would have nothing left to trade. With a heavy heart she ran home, firmly closing her hand around the banana she had been able to get.

Even before she reached her poor abode she heard Dalitso cry, "Mama! Mama!" And when Khaya breathlessly pushed open the door, her sister shrieked, "Mama? Mama? Why are you so cold?"

With a few big strides Khaya stood beside Dalitso and looked at her mother, who lay motionless on her bed with closed eyes. She grabbed her mother's hand and immediately let it fall again.

It was true! The neighbor had been right. Terror-stricken, Khaya stood like one paralyzed, unable to think.

Jabulani, who was not even a year old, became hungry. His crying woke Khaya from her numbness. Although she was only seven she realized that as the oldest she was now responsible for her younger siblings. What should she do? "Jesus, help us!" she cried inwardly.

Pastor Mutowa! The thought flashed through her like lightning. Pastor Mutowa and his wife had come again and again during the last months when her mother had been so sick that she couldn't work anymore. They had brought them Sadza[35] and some vegetables. Surely they would now help them and tell her what to do. Maybe they knew of a position where Khaya could work to feed herself and her siblings.

"Come, Dalitso!" Khaya lifted Jabulani up from the floor and strapped him to her back. "Come, let's go. We can't stay here alone." She took the four-year-old by the hand and pulled her out of the stuffy room into the blazingly bright summer day.

Now, in December, which means summer in the southern hemisphere, the sun stood high in the sky and burned down mercilessly onto the streets where hardly any shade could be found. Again and again Dalitso stopped and wailed, "I'm so hot! I can't go on walking. And I'm so thirsty!"

But Khaya determinedly pulled her along. An inner urge drove her on. It wouldn't have helped anyway to sit at the

---

[35] corn mush

side of the road in the scorching sun. Only once, when one lonely tree gave a little shade, she allowed herself and her sister a few minutes of rest. But soon she urged her on.

At last they reached the church building. But the door was locked. Khaya squatted down with Dalitso and Jabulani as close as possible to the building to take advantage of the little strip of shade. Jabulani again began to cry, Dalitso whimpered quietly, but Khaya gritted her teeth and stared down in front of her.

Not long afterwards, light steps came near. Then a well-known voice asked, "Khaya! Why are you here at this time of the day? In the heat of noon? Is something wrong with your mother?"

The sympathetic words of the pastor's wife released Khaya from her numbness. She burst into desperate tears. "Our mother's dead," she gasped out with difficulty. "We're all alone!"

"Oh, you poor children!" Mrs. Mutowa bent down and lifted Jabulani into her arms. Then she tenderly stroked the girls' hair. "Come with me! I think the first thing you need is something to eat and drink."

Swallowing hard to suppress her sobbing, Khaya, with her head bent, slowly followed the pastor's wife, clasping Dalitso's hand. At the side of the church they entered the little house, where the pastoral couple now lived alone, after all four of their children had gotten married and moved out.

While the girls satisfied their hunger and thirst, Mrs. Mutowa fed the little boy. Then she suggested, "I need to go and decorate the church as tomorrow is Christmas. Would you like to come along and help?"

As she had expected, the work diverted the girls' thoughts from their grief at least for a little while. The baby slept on a blanket on the floor near the altar where Mrs. Mutowa could see him. With sad, serious faces, but willingly, the two girls followed the instructions, and after some time the whole church glittered and gleamed in colorful, festive decorations.

For dinner the pastor's wife cooked Mutakura[36] and served red beets with it. For a long time the children hadn't had anything that good, and so they ate their fill despite their grief.

After the meal Pastor Mutowa cleared his throat and looked at the girls. "Khaya, Dalitso, and you too, Jabulani,"–he smiled at the little boy who sat fed and therefore content on his wife's lap-and again turned to the girls. "Your mother's body is cared for. While you decorated the church, I took care of a proper burial for her. But you now have no relatives at all; you actually have nobody any more. You're totally alone. That's why I want to ask you: Would you like to stay with us? As our children? We don't have much ourselves, but God has never let us down. He will surely help us to care for you."

Khaya kneaded her hands in her lap. That was not what she had expected. She had hoped for some advice, maybe a helpful word to somebody who could employ her. But this? This sounded too good to be true. Did he really mean it? They were not related to him, not at all! She lifted her head and questioningly looked at the man who at this moment seemed to her like an angel from heaven.

Pastor Mutowa smiled at her. "Yes, Children, we mean it exactly like I said. Tomorrow is Christmas. We will celebrate that God has given us his son as a gift. And this year he gave us three children at once on top of it. Would you like that? To live with us like our own children?"

With big eyes Khaya first looked at the pastor, then at his wife, who nodded to her, smiling. She swallowed hard. "Yes," she then said quietly, "yes, we would like to stay. You're so good to us! And we don't know where else we could go. If you really want to keep us, we'd love to stay! Thank you! Thank you so very much!" And even more quietly she added, "Thank you, Jesus! Oh, thank you!"

She drew a very deep breath, and for the first time on this day the despair left her eyes.

---

[36] Beans with black-eyed peas

20: Binoy
Naogaon, Bangladesh – ca. 2004

It had been a long day. Binoy (BEE-noy) was walking home with the goat—the one goat that his family owned. Recently the weather had become cooler, and he shivered in his short trousers and the thin shirt. Last spring he had turned nine, so now he was the one who had to care for the goat. Nayan (NAH-yahn), sixteen years old and his oldest brother, worked as a day laborer in the fields to add some extra income for the family. The two brothers, their parents and their other siblings lived in a small Shantal village near Naogaon (NOW-gown) in the north of Bangladesh.

Mmm, this smells good! As Binoy drew nearer to his home, the smell of lentil soup increased. Obviously his mother was preparing their evening meal. His stomach started rumbling. His last meal had been in the early morning. He quickened his pace and stepped into the mud-and-bamboo hut. His mother had used plant juice to paint delicate patterns onto the smooth walls. But Binoy ignored the artwork; he was too hungry and eagerly looked forward to the hearty meal.

Minoti (mee-NOH-tee) and Shefali (shay-FAH-lee), his younger sisters, were playing with dolls that their mother had made for them out of mud and leftover cloth. Their mother was bending over a large clay pot resting above an open fire and filling small bowls made from coconut shells with lentil stew and rice. Each of the family members had their own bowl. They washed their hands and then sat on the floor cross-legged.

Their father and Nayan had come home a short while before Binoy. Now the father thanked their new God for the good meal, and then everybody started eating. Skillfully Binoy formed little balls of rice and lentils with his right hand and shoved them into his mouth. Oh, how delicious!

With his stomach full and his hunger gone, Binoy took a deep breath, licked his lips and leaned back, gazing at his family around him. Two more should have been sitting there, but they had died as infants. Binoy had never met them, as they had been born after Nayan and died before Binoy was born. But for a few years now the health worker from the Christian church had been visiting the village regularly, and since then a lot less babies had died. Not only Minoti and Shefali, now six and three years old, had survived. Also Nipen (NEE-pehn), eight months old and the youngest member of the family, appeared healthy and strong enough to live.

Soon after the evening meal the whole family lay down to sleep on mats made from palm leaves. Tomorrow would be a special day! For the first time, the family wanted to participate in the Christmas celebration at the Christian church that had been established two years ago in the bigger neighboring village.

The next morning the whole family put on the clothes that the mother had washed in the pond the previous day. Minoti even had a new dress. As she helped her little sister dress, she watched her mother wrapping herself in the nicer and newer of her two saris. Plastic bracelets jingled on her wrist.

In single file, the family made their way to the neighboring village, walking on small, narrow paths through rice fields, past sugar cane and corn stalks as tall as a man. The Christians had announced they would gather for the Christmas service in the inner court of the church's Child Development Center. When they were still a little ways off, Binoy and his family could already hear cheerful Christmas carols. All through the month of December they had been singing them with enthusiasm and anticipation, and every time they had sounded even more glad and cheerful.

The walls of the center were decorated with colorful paper. Binoy followed his father and Nayan to the right side where the men were standing, while Minoti and Shefali, with their mother holding Nipen, joined the women on the left side. Soon they were all singing and clapping to the song's rhythm.

After the singing they all sat down cross-legged. Then the program began. Minoti took part in several of the short dramas which the children of the center had been practicing for weeks. Shefali looked on with a bit of envy: She longed for her fifth birthday to arrive, after which she would finally be allowed to go to the center every day with her older sister. Minoti had told her so much about the games and stories and other exciting things.

Binoy was gazing at the tiny mud hut standing on a table in the front. The straw on the floor of the little hut indicated that the divine baby had been put in a manger after his birth. Binoy could hardly see the straw from where he sat. So he watched the plays and other presentations with interest and excitedly joined in the games. Finally the pastor started his Christmas sermon. He told about Joseph and Mary: how they had traveled such a long way, and then nobody would offer them a place to stay; how at last a man had said they could use his stable; and how the divine child had been born, right next to the animals. God himself had come to earth as a baby, not in a bright and sparkling palace, but poor and lowly in a dirty stable. And then the pastor explained, "This God-baby, this Jesus, wants to come to everybody who is ready to open his heart to him and let him live there."

Fascinated, Binoy stared at the pastor. For the first time he was starting to understand the story about this new God, in whom his parents had believed for several months now, and what they had been trying to convey to their children.

After the service everybody gathered for the Christmas dinner: chapati[37] with pork curry and sweet rice pudding for dessert. But Binoy wasn't thinking about the food at all. He was still wondering about what the pastor had said. Was it also true for him? Did Jesus want to come and live in his heart?

---

[37] Flat round bread made from wheat flour, water, and a little salt

And then he suddenly felt sure. "Yes, Jesus," he whispered, "you mean me too! I want to open my heart and let you live there. Thank you that you came down to earth for me, too."

A great, wonderful joy flooded through him. With a bright smile on his face he joined the people standing in line for the food. Now he could properly enjoy the delicious Christmas dinner!

21: Flavia
Cuernavaca, Mexico – ca. 2001

As high as a house, the poinsettia towered above the little hut in the back of the Mendoza family's yard. Yesterday, while the sun was shining, the upper leaves–as large as carriage wheels–had shone in a beautiful dark red color. But early this morning, as Flavia left the hut, only the outline of the huge bush was silhouetted against the dimly lit sky. Sighing, she closed the door to the hut that had been her new home now for only a few days. Her thoughts dwelt at home in the Indian village of the Nahua tribe and with her family. Oh, she'd rather be with her mother now, helping her with the preparations for the Christmas dinner, cooking Pozole, the traditional Christmas corn soup. But as she had turned sixteen recently she was now old enough to help her family financially and earn her own living. So she did what many girls from her village had done before; she moved to Cuernavaca to work as a household help in a Mexican family.

While she was thinking about her parents and siblings who had to work so hard for their daily bread, suddenly a warning rattle reached her ear from one side. Without even looking in the direction of the sound she dashed to the family's house that rose two-storied before her in the gray dawn. Quickly she banged the door shut behind her, leaned against it and closed her eyes, trembling all over.

A rattlesnake! Here in town! In the yard! Flavia knew the horrible nightmare that happened to anyone who was bitten by this highly poisonous snake. *And I have to go back to my hut in the darkness tonight. How can I reach the hut without being attacked by the snake? And don't I have to warn the family?* She had immediately taken a liking to Yolanda, the youngest of the four children. What if she played in the yard and got bitten? Would not she, Flavia, be responsible if the little one died in agony?

Still trembling Flavia left the door and stumbled into the kitchen. Elda, the family's household help for several years, was already working there. As she was planning to get married soon she was teaching Flavia to take her place. She still lived with her family in one of the few poor sections of town. Mainly well-to-do Mexicans lived in Cuernavaca, the "town of eternal spring."

When Flavia entered the kitchen Elda looked up. "At last; it's time you were coming. But oh, what's wrong with you? You're trembling!"

"There...back there...in the yard," Flavia faltered, and her shaking finger pointed to the back door, "there's a rattlesnake, and..."

"Nonsense!" Elda interrupted. "They don't come into town. During all these years I've never seen one. Don't be so silly! Come and help with breakfast. We've a lot to do today."

Not daring to contradict her, Flavia obeyed. But she could not stop thinking about the rattling noise in the yard. The thought followed her after breakfast as she dusted the furniture. She tried to be very careful, despite being in a hurry, so that she wouldn't break any of the carvings on the expensive furniture that was handmade from pine wood.

For a few moments she stopped in front of the colorfully decorated Christmas tree and stared at it. Christmas–the day when the birth of baby Jesus was celebrated! Jesus was God's son. Shouldn't he be able to protect them from the danger? "Oh Jesus, help us!" she whispered. "Please, make that snake go away and leave the yard!"

After Flavia had carefully cleaned everything Elda had told her to, she ironed the formal dresses for Señora Mendoza and her daughters. In the afternoon Elda took her along when she went shopping. As they crossed the front yard to reach the gate, Flavia looked all around her and listened intently. But in the noise of this busy day such a sound would be swallowed up anyway.

Side by side they rushed down the street to the stores. In many places cords were strung across the street. Piñatas, clay pots wrapped in colorful crepe paper or decorated figurines made from cardboard paper, hung from the cords. People were singing, and blindfolded children tried to break the star-shaped figurines. If they succeeded, fruit and sweets fell out which the children collected jubilantly.

When Elda and Flavia entered the first store they were met by Christmas music. Elda quickly selected the ingredients for Ponche Navideño, the traditional Mexican Christmas punch: oranges, guavas, and, of course, tejocotes[38], raisins, walnuts and additional fruits, as well as candy canes.

Then they rushed on to the fish store to buy bacalao–cod. They needed cod to mix with olives, raisins and spices to make the typical Christmas salad.

The more Elda and Flavia neared the Mendoza family's home on their way back the more nervous Flavia became. While shopping and seeing all those exciting things the shock of the morning had moved to the back of her consciousness. But now it all came back. Would the baby Jesus have heard her plea?

As soon as they entered the house they heard agitated voices. Andres and Sergio, the two sons, were shouting at the same time. In between they recognized the high voices of Señora Mendoza and Maria-Elena, the older daughter, and once in a while also the deep voice of Señor Mendoza. Only Yolanda's soft voice was missing. Was it only because the others were louder? Or...?

Flavia's heart beat rapidly while she followed Elda into the kitchen. Had something happened to Yolanda? Had the snake bitten her? Flavia had a hard time concentrating on the preparations for the festive meal. The turkey had to be stuffed and put into the oven so that it would be ready for the big meal later in the evening. The ingredients for the punch and the cod salad were waiting to be washed, peeled, cut, and whatever else was necessary. The family would first go to the Catholic church for the Christmas service that started at six. But as Yolanda was still quite

---

[38] The Mexican hawthorn

small they wanted the meal served two hours earlier than the usual time of eleven. And Flavia would be allowed to serve at table.

Before the family left for the service Sergio rushed into the kitchen. "We've got a rattlesnake in the yard!" he shouted. "But Papá killed it!"

"Did the snake bite Señorita Yolanda?" Flavia wanted to ask. But her voice failed her. Elda shot a quick glance at Flavia and then turned to Sergio. "Was anybody bitten?"

"No." Sergio shook his head. Then he tapped his chest and announced, "I saw it first and called Papá right away."

Flavia closed her eyes and breathed deeply. Her prayer had been heard. The danger was gone. Relief flooded her from head to toe. With new energy she peeled the oranges for the punch.

After the family returned from church Yolanda came quietly into the kitchen. She tugged at Flavia's dress and gave her a small picture. "Look," she explained, "this is baby Jesus in the manger. And that is the Virgin Mary and Joseph." Her little finger pointed at the colorful scrawling. "And the ox and the donkey. And up there are the angels. They sing *Glory to God in the highest and peace on earth*. I drew this picture for you so that you can celebrate Christmas, too."

Warm joy flooded through Flavia. "Gracias, Señorita Yolanda," she whispered and bent down to the child. "Thank you so much!"

22: Marit
Kiruna, Northern Sweden – ca. 1995

"Today is JuleEve!" Mikael considered it his responsibility to inform his little sister Marit. He was sure the four-year-old could not remember last year's Christmas Eve. It had been a whole year!

"Oh, nice!" Marit clapped her hands. "Then Juletomte (yule TOHM-tah) will come today with his reindeer sleigh and bring nice presents!"

"Who told you such nonsense?" Mikael with his seven years of age thought himself very old and wise because he no longer believed in Santa Claus. "There is no Juletomte. It's only a fairy tale that people have invented. The presents are put under the tree by Mommy and Daddy."

Marit looked at her big brother frowning. Could this be true? Then she danced over to her mother and plucked at her skirt. "Where is Daddy? When will Daddy finally come home?"

"Daddy went to see patients. He wants to check on the elderly and bring them a nice Christmas greeting, you know? A small bag with the gingerbread we baked yesterday. Do you remember?"

"Oh, yes!" Marit passionately nodded her head. She certainly hadn't forgotten how busily she had helped cutting out the different shapes, and how good the kitchen had smelled when the gingerbread came out of the oven. That she had just as busily fought with her brother to get the nicest cookie cutters–that fact she had speedily deleted from her memory.

"What're you doing?" she now asked.

"Preparing the special meal for tonight."

"Mmm, will there be ham again? The one with the sweet mustard crust?" Mikael smacked his lips.

"Of course! And red cabbage, and herring salad, and all the other good things that belong to a real good Christmas meal," the mother confirmed. "But don't interrupt me now. It's already past noon, and I still have lots to do."

"Come, Marit!" Mikael took her hand. "We'll go and look out of the window to see whether Daddy's coming." He helped her push a chair to the window and climb up onto it. Then he stood beside her.

"Yes, children, look out for Daddy," their mother agreed. "He should be home any moment now." She turned back to her preparations. Although they had been living up here in the north in Kiruna in the Norrbotten province since last summer, she still wanted to prepare their usual Christmas feast as they had been used to it when they lived in Jönköping (YOON-koo-ping) in the south of Sweden.

Marit didn't remain on her chair for long. She glided down, tripped over to her mother and complained, "Out there it's almost always dark now! For soooo long already! Won't it be light again sometime?"

"Yes, Mommy," Mikael joined in from the window. "How much longer will it take until at last it'll get really light again? Not just such a blue twilight, but really bright daylight? I so long for real sunshine again!"

"I do, too," the mother agreed. "But so far north the polar night does take several weeks."

"Weeks? Oh my! Why did we move up here in the first place?"

"Why, Mommy?" Marit crossed her hands behind her back and looked up at her mother.

"Because Jesus sent us here so that Daddy can help the sick people and tell them about Jesus. There aren't too many medical doctors among the Sami here in Lapland. They also need medical help. But now leave me alone; or I won't be ready on time. Daddy must be home any moment now!"

"Oh yes!" Marit ran back to the window and knelt on her chair. In harmony the siblings looked out into the early afternoon. The snow shone and glittered in the light of the street lamps. Once in a while a snowmobile passed by; apart from that everything was quiet. No sound was heard from the rail line that ran from Luleå (LOO-lay-oh) at the Baltic Sea to Narvik (NAR-vik) at the Atlantic Ocean in Norway and passed through Kiruna to pick up the iron ore that was mined here. The Nordkalottvägen (NORD-kah-lot-VAY-gehn), the big road from Kiruna to Narvik, that in summer brought troops of tourists into town, was too far away from their home to be noticed.

"Mommy, will we go up to the tip of Kebnekaise (KAYB-neh-KY-zeh) some day?" Mikael turned around to his mother. "Daddy said it's the highest mountain in all of Sweden, more than sixty-six hundred feet high!"

The mother laughed a little without looking up from her work. "Yes, someday we'll probably climb Kebnekaise, since we live right next to it. But surely not now in winter. For that we'll need bright daylight and..."

A cry interrupted her. "Look, Mommy! Look, look!" Marit shrieked and tapped her finger at the windowpane.

The mother dropped her knife and rushed to the window. "What's wrong?"

"There, there!" Marit shouted and pointed at a group of Sami women who were plodding through the snow in their full native costume. Multicolored embroidery on wide red ribbons adorned the tightly woven material of the dresses at the hems of the skirts and the borders of the sleeves. But in the weak light the embroidery was hardly visible. Only the white parts, as well as the white knitted gloves, shone against the dark cloth of the garments.

"Why do you call me for that? I'm sure they wear their traditional costumes today because this is a feast day. Have you never seen them like this?"

"No, Mommy, but look what they're wearing on their heads. It looks so different from my cap!"

"That's just their way of knitting their caps—everybody the way he or she likes it. They're pretty with their embroidery, don't you think?"

"Oh yes, and I want one of those caps!"

"I heard that in February there'll be a market around here where they sell these handcrafted things. We could go there and look for them. But now let me continue.

Otherwise the meal won't be ready on time." She threw a glance at the clock and then turned back to her preparations. Why hadn't Gunnar (GOO-nar) come home yet?

"It's snowing again, Mommy," Mikael announced a while later.

"It's snowing again, Mommy," Marit echoed, imitating the tone of her brother.

"Copycat!" Mikael murmured. Loudly he asked, "When is Daddy finally coming home?"

"Hopefully soon!" The mother again glanced at the clock with a worried look.

"There's Daddy!" Marit shouted and pointed to a snowmobile that was drawing nearer fast.

"Nonsense, that's not Daddy. Daddy's much taller," Mikael corrected his little sister.

For some time they stared out of the window silently. The snow fell more and more densely. They could hardly see the light of the nearest street lamp through the white glitter. Then it started howling around the house.

"Are those wolves?" Marit grabbed her brother's hand.

"Nonsense, that's just the wind, Silly." Mikael pushed the little hand away.

For a while there was silence between the two siblings. Then Marit asked, "When will we finally dance around the Christmas tree? You said we'll dance around the tree when it's fully decorated."

"Only after we've eaten," Mikael explained.

"And when are we gonna eat?"

"When Daddy has come back!"

"And when will Daddy be back?"

"How should I know that?" Mikael growled.

"I'm so bored," Marit grumbled.

"Well, get out your Legos and build something nice," the mother suggested.

Several hours later the table was set with all the good things the mother had prepared. Even the rice pudding with the hidden almond in it wasn't missing. Only the father still wasn't home.

"When is Daddy finally coming home?" Marit complained. "I'm hungry!"

"Be quiet!" Mikael punched her in the side and then looked at his mother out of the corner of his eye. He sensed her growing uneasiness about his father not being home yet.

The mother tightened her shoulders. "Don't quarrel, children! Come, let's pray to Jesus that he..."

Before she could finish her sentence, the deep purring of a snowmobile could be heard and died a moment later in front of the house. "That's Daddy!" Marit shouted, ran to the front door, tore it open and in the next moment threw herself at her father.

"Thank you, Lord!" the mother murmured. She looked at her husband, a question in her eyes. "You're so late, Gunnar!"

First, he lifted Marit up and whirled her through the air so that she screeched and laughed. "You won't believe what happened!"

"What? What? Tell us!" the children pressed.

"I saw the Christ Child!"

"Oh! Where? Where? I wanna see it too!" Marit jumped up and down.

The father first turned to his wife and said in a low voice, "Way over on the other side of Nordkalottvägen somebody was in a very great hurry to show up in this world, and there were some complications. That's why I'm so late. I'm sorry, Ragna[39]!"

Then he squatted down in front of Marit. "I was there when a little boy was born today. Right on Christmas Eve. Like baby Jesus long ago!" He straightened himself up. "And now let's eat. I'm quite hungry after being out so long in the fresh air on the snowmobile. Let's see who will find the almond in the rice-pudding tonight!" And he winked at his wife.

---

[39] pronounced RAHG-nah

23: Govind
Mumbai, India – 1998

Govind (go-vind) bent down and picked up another plastic bag. He felt so tired. But then he spotted an old newspaper rustling in the wind. Hurriedly he stooped down and grabbed it before the wind could blow it away. Beside him the traffic rushed back and forth. The loud honking of the many horns even rose above the roar of the car engines. Rusty, rumbling buses tried to pass rattling trucks. A few Indian passenger cars worked their way through the mess, honking constantly. Lots of three-wheelers pushed themselves in-between, pulling a black tail of stinking exhaust behind them. They always found a tiny gap, and often not even a hand could be squeezed in between them and their neighboring car.

Govind coughed from all the exhaust and the dust the cars raised. The road had been built for four lanes, but the drivers transformed it into a six or eight lane road. It was one of the main roads in this part of the city, and it led to downtown Mumbai[40]. But Govind had never been downtown. He didn't know that every year the number of inhabitants grew by more than half a million, and that by now Mumbai had become the biggest city, not only of India, but of the whole world.

For Govind had never attended a school. He could neither read nor write. He didn't even know that he was eight years old, as he had never heard about calendars. He knew that winter was approaching only because he wasn't sweating as much as he had a few weeks earlier. Though, to be exact, he couldn't count weeks either. And nobody had ever told him about months, and that this one was called December by the world. He couldn't go to school because he had to help earn money. He and his mother

---

[40] New name of Bombay

and even Sunita (soo-NEE-tah), his five-year-old little sister, went along the roads to collect old cans, newspapers, and plastic bags. These they sold to a dealer and got a few rupees for the trash. His father, who had worked as a day laborer building or tearing down houses, had left the family more than a year ago. Since then they had even less money for food and clothing.

While Govind trudged along the road on his bare feet and collected trash, his thoughts traveled back to lunch. Like always it had consisted of a few flat round cakes of bread which his mother had baked from sorghum flour. And she had cooked some curry from potatoes and pulse. But it had not satisfied Govind's stomach. The reason, however, why he thought about lunch was not connected to food. At that time a visitor had entered their little hut made out of metal sheets. A woman wearing a sari without a single hole or tear had come in and invited the family to a special festivity. She had called it Christmas. And it was to be celebrated over in the better part of Kanjur Slum where they had real little houses built from stone, and where the people could afford tidy clothing. They bought their saris and shirts from the dealers who bought them from rich people when the rich people didn't want them anymore.

This evening Govind would be allowed to go to the festivity. With new vigor he bent down and picked up a dusty can. Soon it would be dark, and he wanted to collect as much trash as possible. Oh yes, and his mother had asked him to bring back some good sturdy twigs for a new broom. The old one was so broken that Sunita couldn't sweep the floor anymore.

After sunset Govind returned to their hut in Kanjur Slum. It was good that the rainy season was over so that the simple homes were no longer flooded. The last puddles had dried, the ground was relatively clean and it didn't stink as much as it did during the summer months. Govind rushed to his home and took Sunita's little hand in his. Since Jeevan, his older brother, had been killed by a truck, Govind was the oldest and felt responsible for his younger sisters. His mother followed them with Chaya (CHAH-yah) in her arms. Because of the lack of proper food, the two-year-old little girl was so weak she could neither sit nor walk.

While the small family picked their way through dogs and chickens, Govind lifted his nose and breathed deeply. Mmm, did that smell good! He didn't know that some people cooked fruit with cinnamon as he had never had the opportunity to taste something that delicious. But the wonderful smell made his mouth water.

He soon forgot the smell when he entered the little stone house and sat on the floor, legs crossed, with lots of other kids. Fascinated, he followed the program the visitor had explained at lunch time. She had introduced herself as the teacher of the new school here in Kanjur Slum. The school was operated by something called a Christian church. Several children from Kanjur Slum attended that school and learned to read and write and calculate. That enabled them to learn a profession when they grew up, and even earn so much money that they could buy enough food and decent clothing.

The school children first sang several songs, and then they enacted a story. A girl named Mary in a white sari was visited by a child called an angel. It had wings fastened on its back. The angel promised a baby to Mary. She and a boy, who wore a white garment, had a white cloth on his head, and was supposed to be her husband, walked to another village. But they couldn't find decent lodging, so they had to stay overnight in a stable.

With big eyes Govind watched. Suddenly there were several of those angels. Other children clothed in long, brown cotton garments, who had long hair and beards, listened attentively to what the angels proclaimed: "God sent his son down onto the earth. He was born in a stable, looks like a small human baby, and he is lying in a manger. That is how you can recognize him."

And then the shepherds jumped up and acted as if they took a little lamb in their arms and took other sheep along. They found the stable, knelt down, and worshipped the baby. As Govind had never seen such a lifelike doll he couldn't understand why the baby didn't move.

More visitors came to see the baby. Three children in shining garments with golden crowns on their heads stepped up to the manger, bowed low in front of the baby and brought presents.

While Govind was still staring at the baby that was supposed to be God's son, a man in tidy black pants and a clean white shirt got up and started to speak. He explained that there is only one God who created all mankind, and who loves all men and women and children. And because he loves them so much he sent his son into the world to help the people and save them from all evil. "God sent his son as the greatest, and best, and most precious gift that was ever given. And to remember that, each child will now also receive a gift."

His mouth wide open, Govind stared at the man. He couldn't believe his ears. In his whole life he had never ever received a gift. His eyes grew bigger and bigger while he watched the school children get new clothes. And with bright shining eyes they said, "Thank you," and didn't need to pay a single rupee.

But the visiting children also got wonderful presents. Speechless with astonishment, Govind held clean pants and a clean shirt in his hands–more beautiful than anything he had ever even touched in his whole life. And in addition to that he got something sweet which melted in his mouth. That was even better than what he had smelled on the way.

But, as he was walking home, what kept his attention was the story. If there really was a God who loved him–Govind–so much that he gave his only son as the best present of all, he desperately wanted to know more about that God.

24: Bela
Bethlehem, Israel – under Roman rule

"Daddy, that foolish sheep has run away again. I counted twice. Both times there were only two hundred and thirty-eight sheep. And I didn't see that one sheep that always runs away."

"Well, I guess we'll have to look for it again, the little rascal." The father sighed und waved to another shepherd. "Jotham, would you please watch our sheep while we're away?"

"Of course, Salmon. Good luck!"

"Thanks!" Salmon and his son Bela walked off. As it was already dark, their search wasn't easy. They had brought a lantern. But it didn't shine very far.

"Why does this crazy sheep do it again and again?"

The father shrugged his shoulders. "Maybe it's especially curious."

"But Daddy! It should've realized by now that it only harms itself. How often it got hurt when it ran away! The other day when it fell into those thorns it was even bleeding."

"You see, Bela, not everyone learns from the consequences of their mistakes. When you were little you didn't want to realize that either."

"That's true. But now I'm big, almost grown up. And even when I was little I understood when you explained something to me. But when I tried to explain to that sheep that it only hurts itself by running away, it just looked at me foolishly. And took the next chance to run off!"

Salmon smiled. "Oh Bela! You didn't really expect the sheep to understand what you said, did you? It might notice from the tone of your voice whether you're angry because you scream at it, or whether you're nice because you speak softly and kindly. But it would only really understand you if you could speak in its sheep language. And you could only understand how a sheep thinks and feels if you became a sheep yourself."

"Oh no, thank you, I'd rather not!" Bela shook his head. No, he preferred to be a normal Hebrew boy.

Meanwhile they had retraced most of the journey they had made during the day. Suddenly Salmon stopped and took hold of Bela's arm. "Listen!"

Bela strained his ears. He couldn't see much as it was completely dark by now. And then he heard it, too: a faint bleating, barely audible.

Slowly Salmon and Bela followed the sound. Again and again they stopped and listened. At last the bleating grew a little louder. A while later they found the runaway by some big rocks. Apparently the little rascal had tried to climb on them, but had fallen and broken a leg.

Bela lifted the sheep into his arms. It was bleating piteously. His father lit the way with the lantern, and they wandered back to the camp. There Bela put the sheep onto a soft fleece and watched as Salmon put the broken leg in sturdy splints. Then they sat down with the other shepherds, covered their shoulders with skins and tried to warm themselves by the fire.

"Isn't it cold tonight?" Bela wrapped the skin more tightly around himself and moved nearer to the fire. Very far above him many, many stars were glistening. And the fire drew a circle of light on the ground. But beyond the circle it was pitch dark. Now and then a tiny light moved through the darkness. That was one of the shepherds checking to see if everything was in order. Here in the mountains of Judah there were lions, and they sometimes liked to devour a sheep if they found nothing else.

For some time Bela blinked up at the stars. "How far away they are," he whispered to himself. "Maybe God lives up there somewhere. The Holy Scriptures say that God is so great that all the heavens cannot contain him. Our famous king Solomon said it when he dedicated the temple he had built for God. But how..."

The next word froze on his tongue. All of a sudden, in the middle of the night, there was a wide strip of light across the sky. It was so bright that it hurt Bela's eyes. And within this light there stood a mighty man. "Don't be afraid!" said the man with a clear, loud voice. "I bring you good news of great joy for everyone! The Savior—yes, the Messiah, the Lord—has been born tonight in Bethlehem, the city of David! And this is how you will recognize him: You will find a baby lying in a manger, wrapped snuggly in strips of cloth!"[41]

Before Bela could recover from his shock something new happened. Although Bela hadn't seen where they came from, the shining light was suddenly filled with hundreds of men. Surely they were angels, for they were clothed in long white robes. And all of them praised God and shouted, "Glory to God in the highest heaven, and peace on earth to all whom God favors!"[42]

After the bright light and the men had disappeared, Bela sat for a long while and stared up into the sky, which had turned dark again. When he felt a strong hand on his shoulder, he started.

"Come, Bela," his father said quietly. "We also want to go and see what has happened. Come! The others have already gone ahead."

Bela felt his father's hand tremble. Slowly he got up and turned around. He felt like one in a dream. Was all of this reality? Without realizing it he slid his hand into his father's big one. Normally he considered himself too grown up for that. But this was a special night, wasn't it?

Salmon pressed Bela's hand. Then he pulled him along. Soon they had caught up with the others. Nobody spoke. There was complete silence. Only sometimes a twig cracked beneath their feet while they hurried along with their lanterns through the dark cold night.

At last they stood in front of the cave that was used as a stable. Once more they looked at each other silently. Then the first one entered and the others followed, slowly, quietly, without talking.

---

[41] according to New Living Translation
[42] according to New Living Translation

It was true! A newborn baby lay in a manger, wrapped in strips of rough cloth. Beside the manger a young woman was lying in the straw. She looked tired and exhausted but she smiled. Behind the manger a young man sat on the floor and looked at the visitors questioningly.

While Jotham explained why they had come, Bela stared at the tiny child. It looked a little red and wrinkled like most newborns. And this was supposed to be Christ, the Savior? The One the prophets had spoken about many centuries ago? Who was to liberate his people?

Bela frowned. It couldn't be true! Or could it? It was exactly like the angels had told them. But just a normal baby? An ordinary human being?

And then–suddenly–he knew why. The little sheep! Like the lost, disobedient sheep! Only if he, Bela, could have become a sheep he could have understood the sheep and been able to help it. And now God had become human–a normal human–to understand humans and help them. How much he must love his people!

Acknowledgments and Resources

As I mentioned at the beginning of the book, several of our native friends and coworkers helped with insightful information. This enabled me to write stories that could have easily taken place like that. So I not only want to thank my husband, my daughter Dorli and my American daughter-in-law Rebekah who put an enormous amount of work into advising me and correcting my drafts, but I want to thank also those precious people whose names I won't mention to protect their identity for security reasons.

Many of those countries I visited myself and saw the situation. I got further information from the following resources:

"Portugal: A Place of Refuge" by M.J. Guerreiro (1999-2000 NWMS Reading Books, Nazarene Publishing House)
ADAC-Series "Das Bild unserer Welt"
Time Life Series "Internationale Speisekarte"
Time Life Series "Die Nationen Europas"
"Die letzten Paradiese der Menschheit" (by Heinrich Harrer, Praesentverlag Heinz Peter)
"UNESCO Naturerbe der Welt" (Weltbild)
"Bright and Shining Revival" by Kathie Walters
"Das Große Bibellexikon" (R.Brockhaus, Brunnen)
"The Zondervan Pictorial Encyclopedia of the Bible"
"The ESV Study Bible"
Internet-Site "Carolship Parade of Lights"
Internet-Site Maori names
Internet-Site Portuguese names